DC
COMICS™

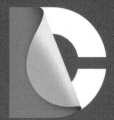

Bedtime for Batman is published by
Picture Window Books
a Capstone imprint
1710 Roe Crest Drive
North Mankato, Minnesota 56003
www.mycapstone.com

STAR36602

Cataloging-in-Publication Data is available on
the Library of Congress website.

ISBN: 978-1-5158-0652-3 (hardcover)
ISBN: 978-1-62370-733-0 (eBook)

Design by Bob Lentz

Printed and bound in China.
009597F16

words by MICHAEL DAHL

pictures by ETHEN BEAVERS

Batman created by BOB KANE with BILL FINGER

BEDTIME FOR BATMAN ™

PICTURE WINDOW BOOKS
a Capstone imprint

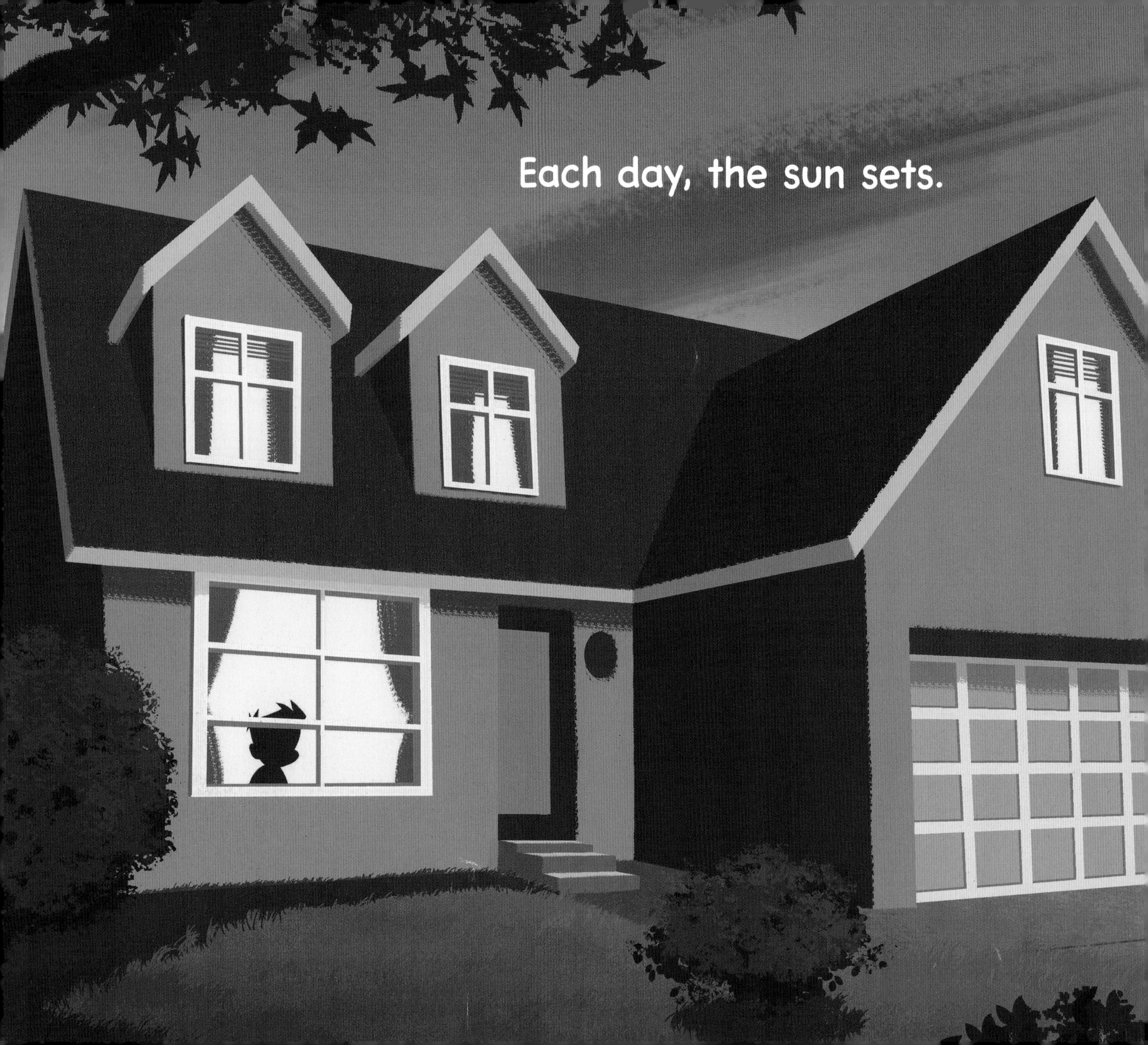

Each day, the sun sets.

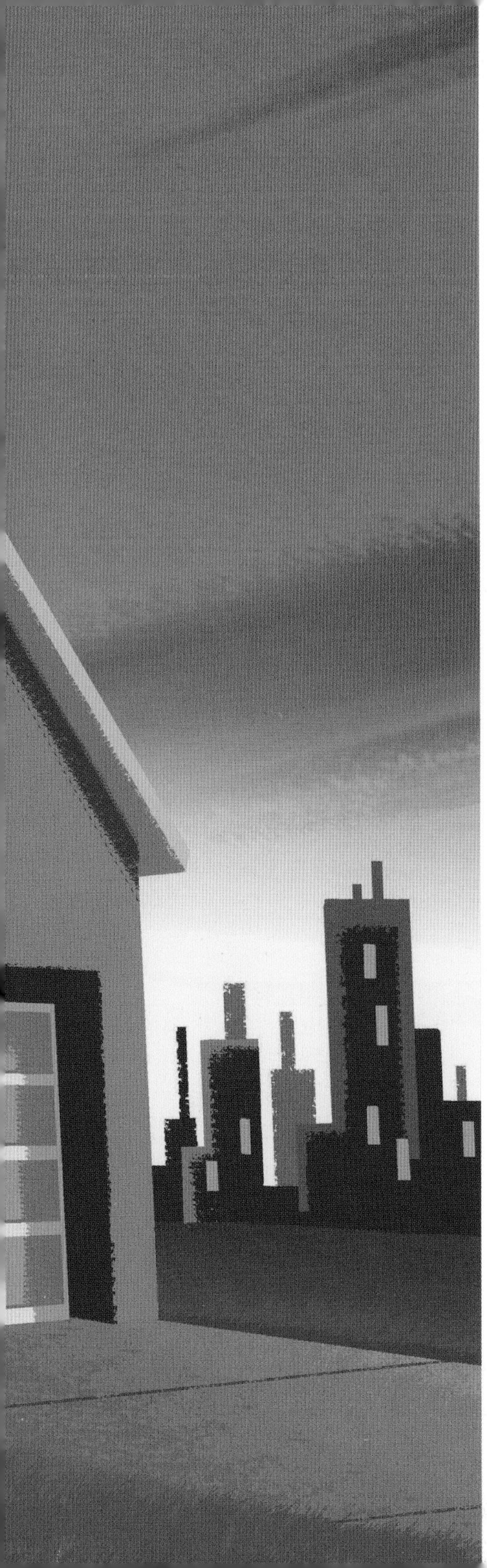

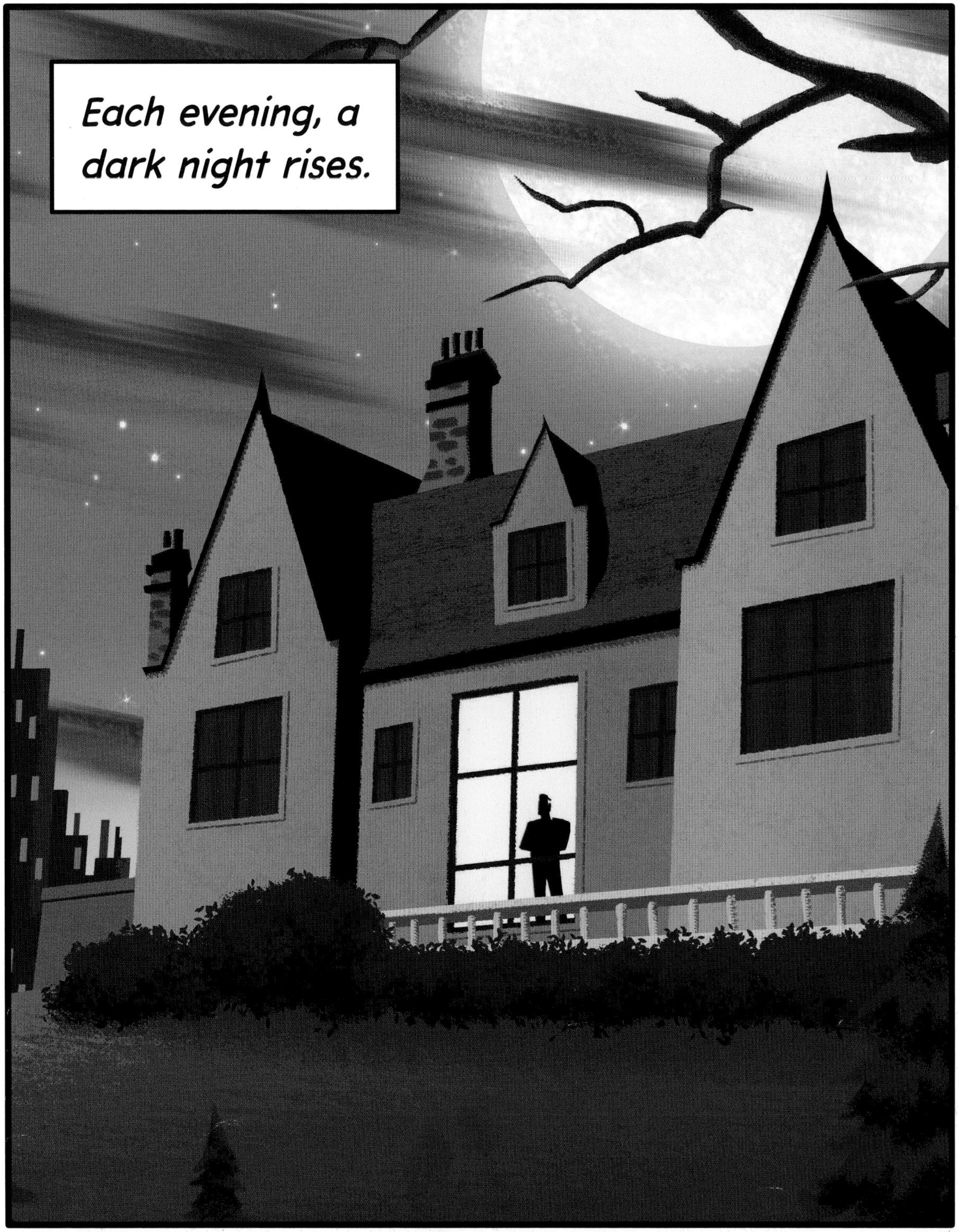
Each evening, a dark night rises.

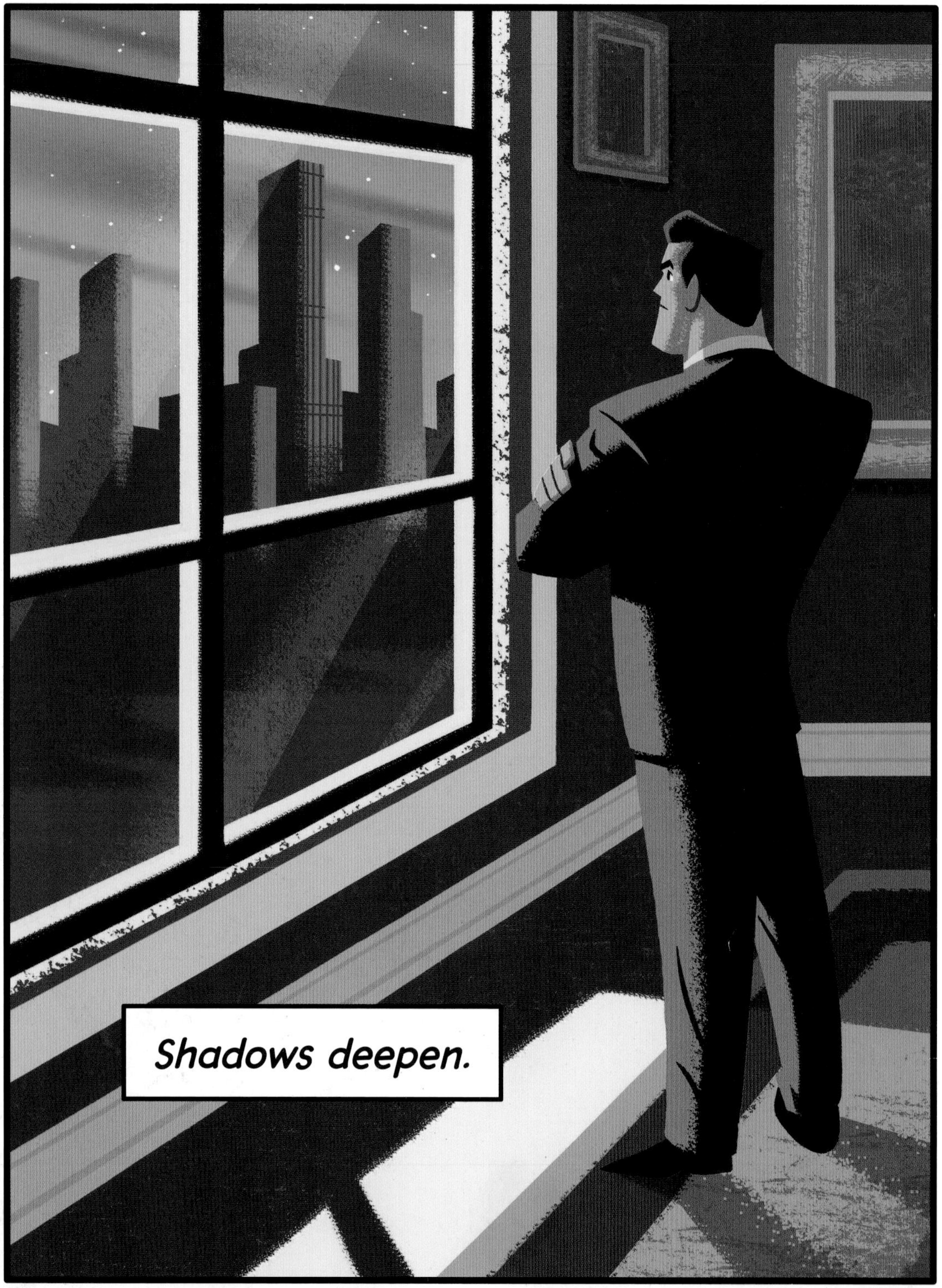
Shadows deepen.

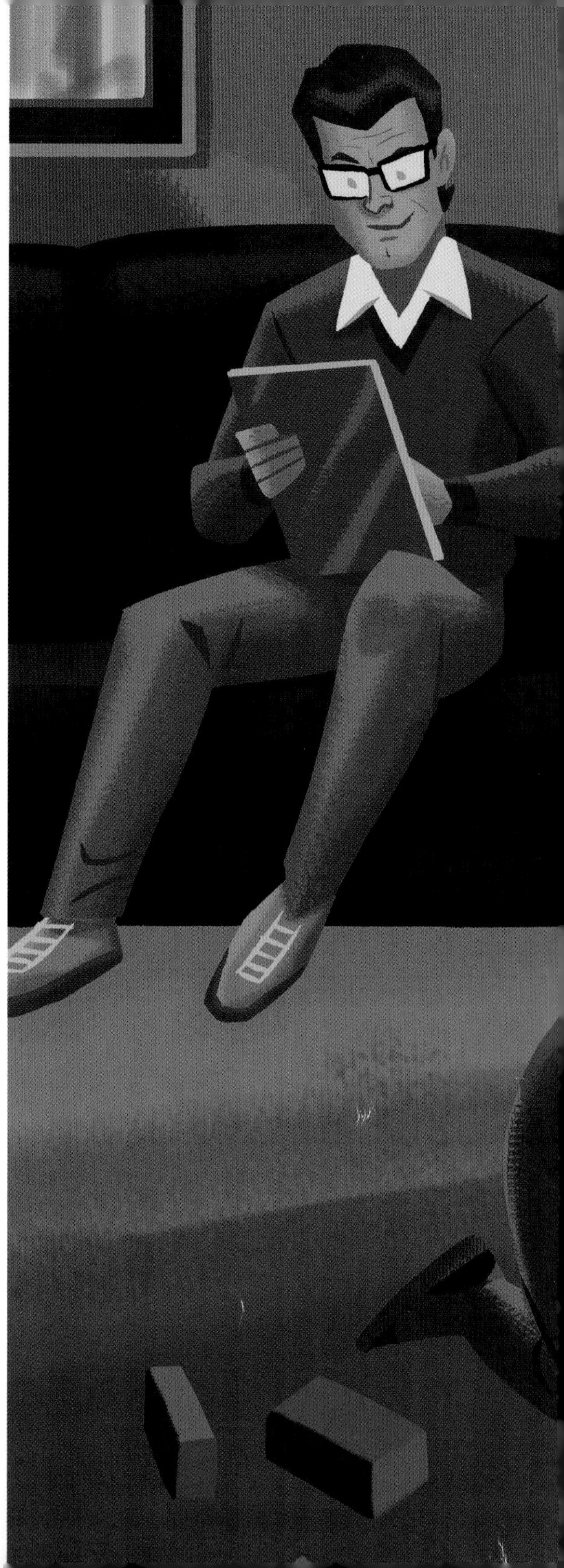

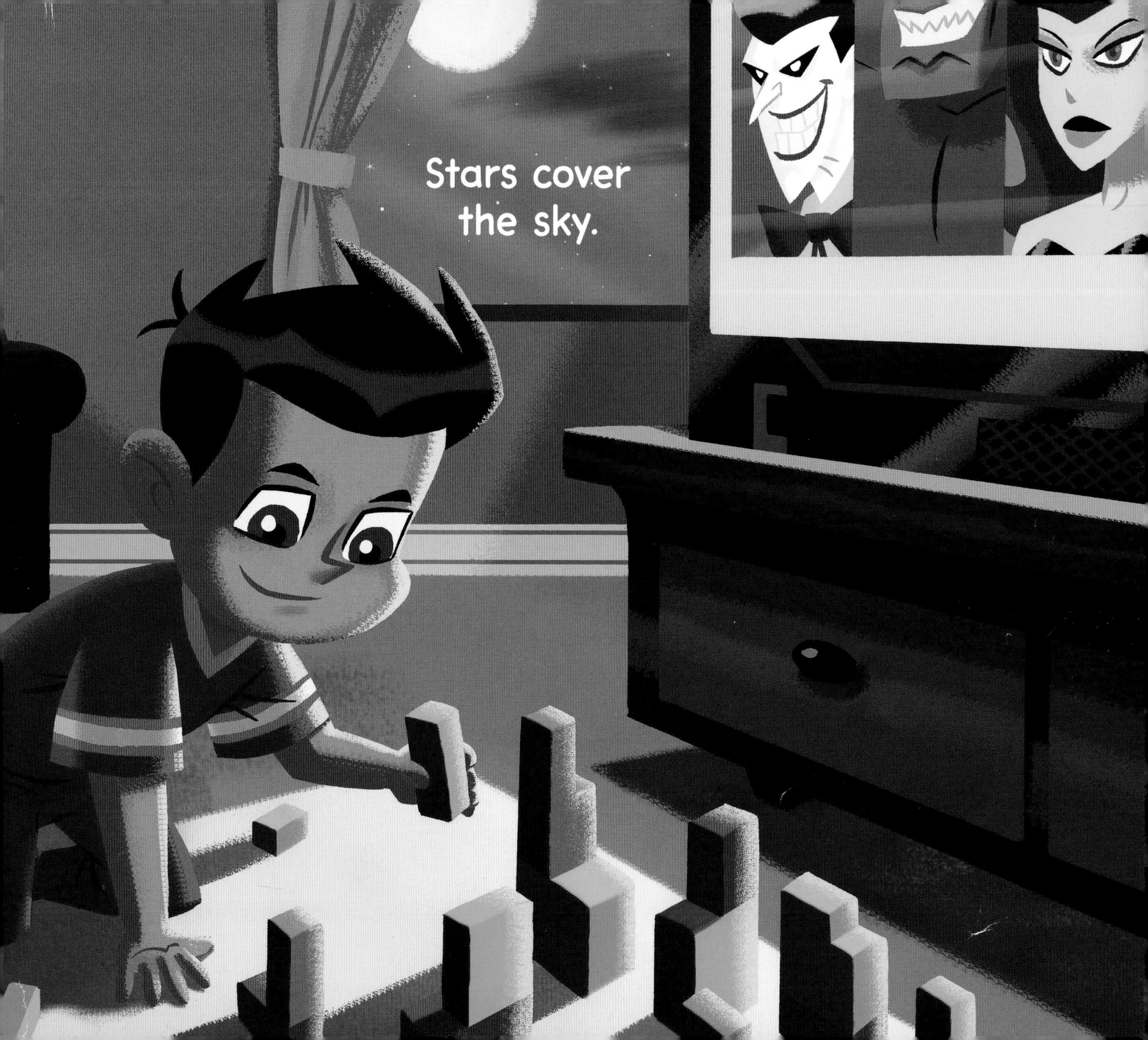

Stars cover
the sky.

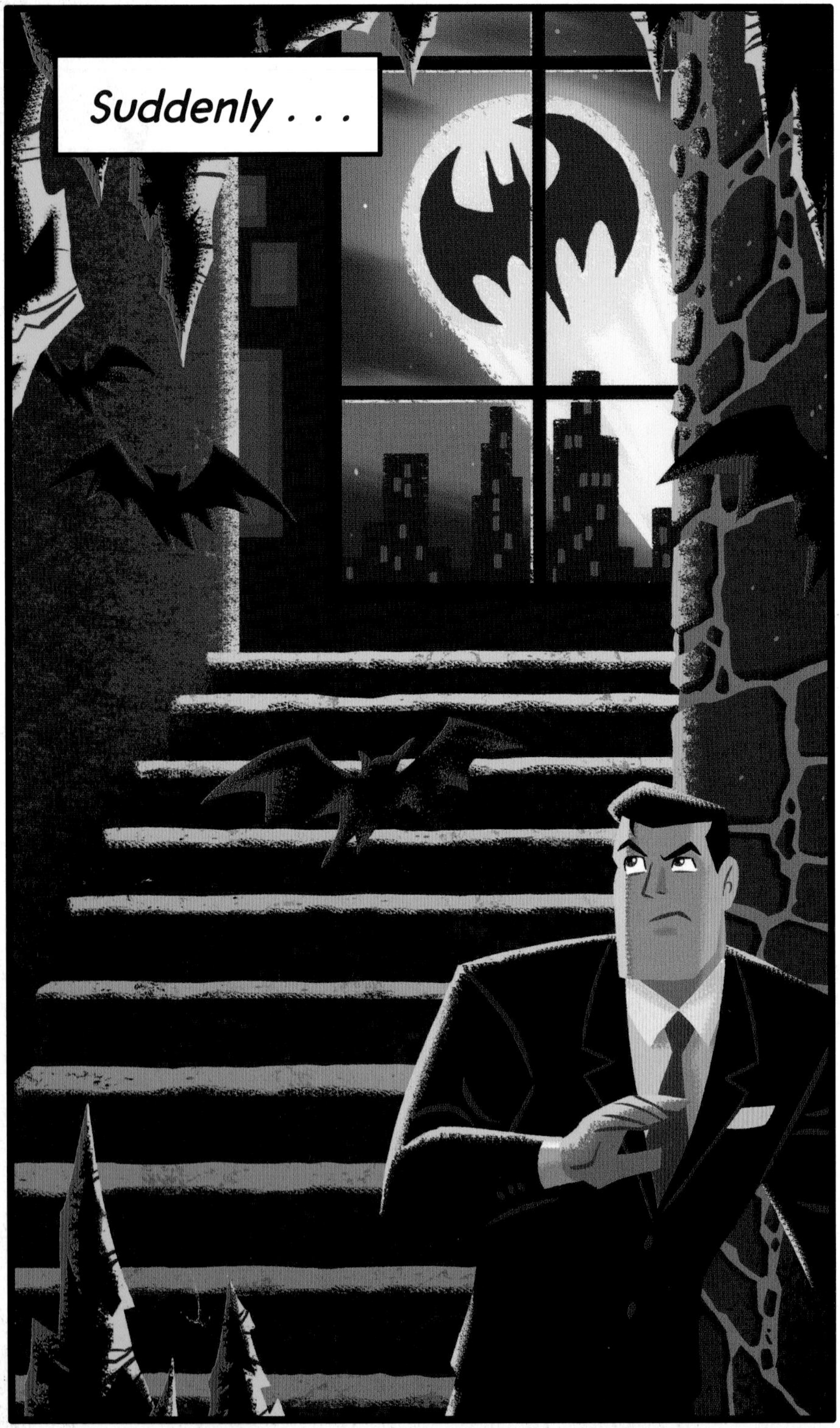
Suddenly . . .

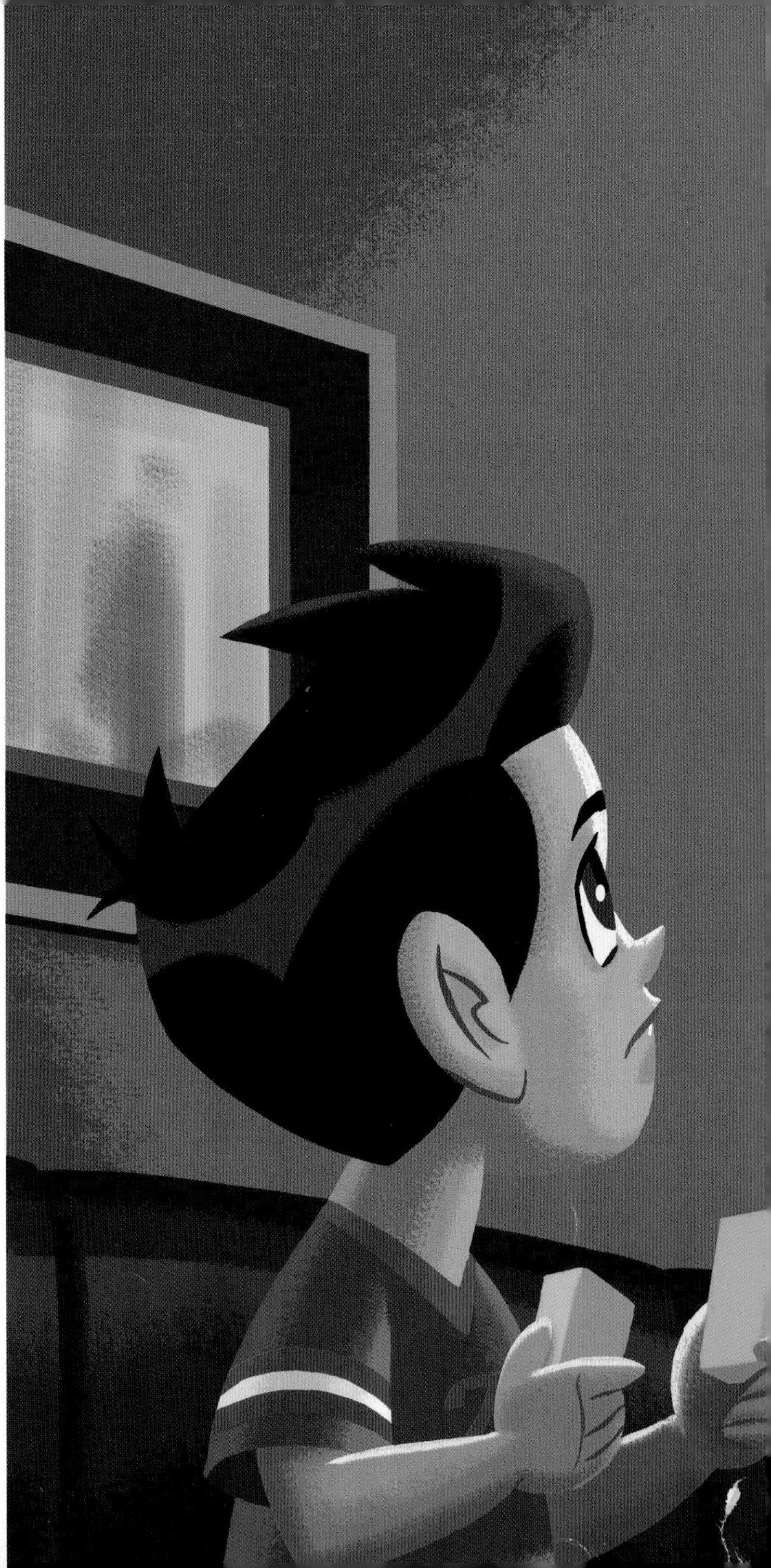

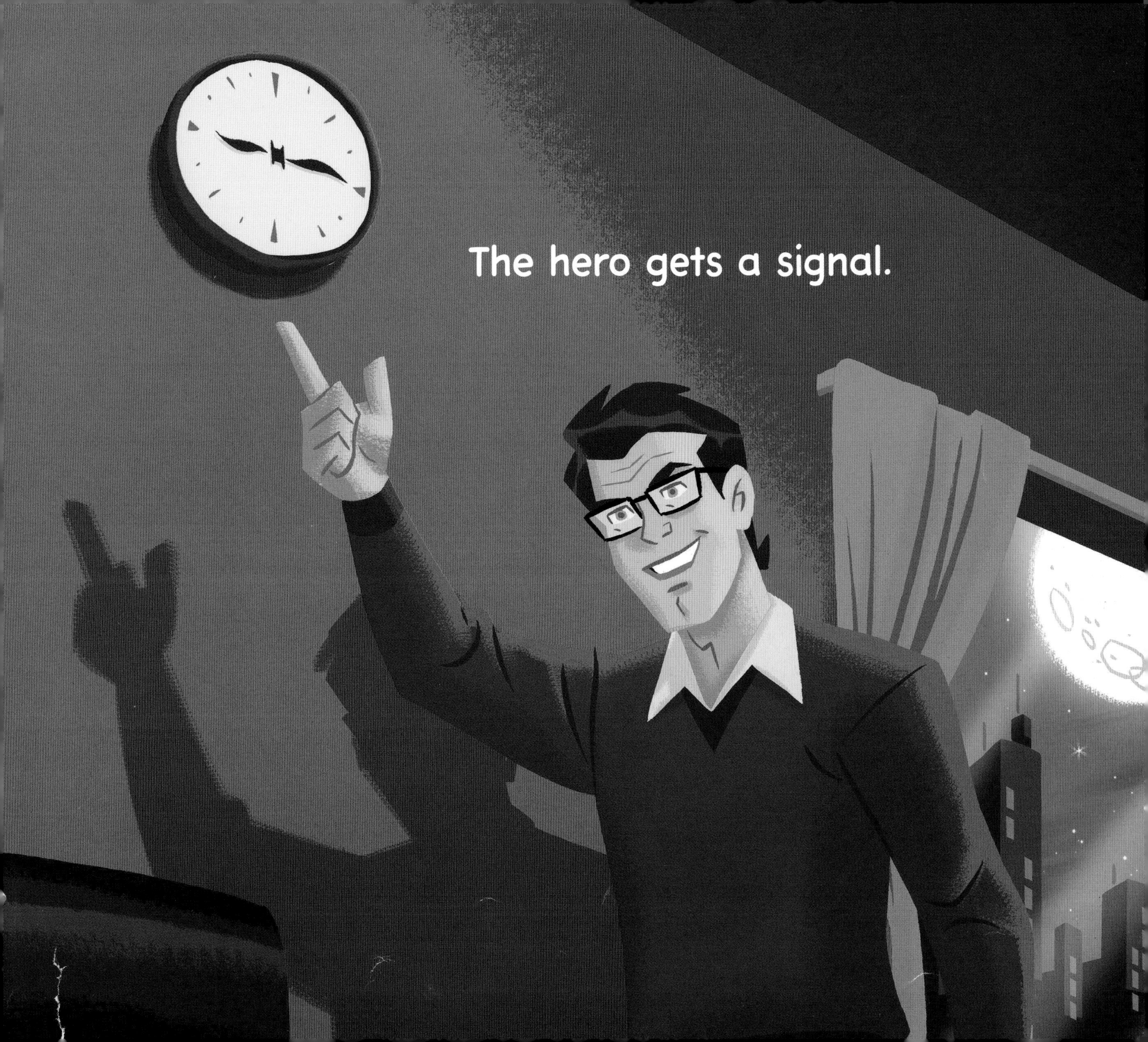

The hero gets a signal.

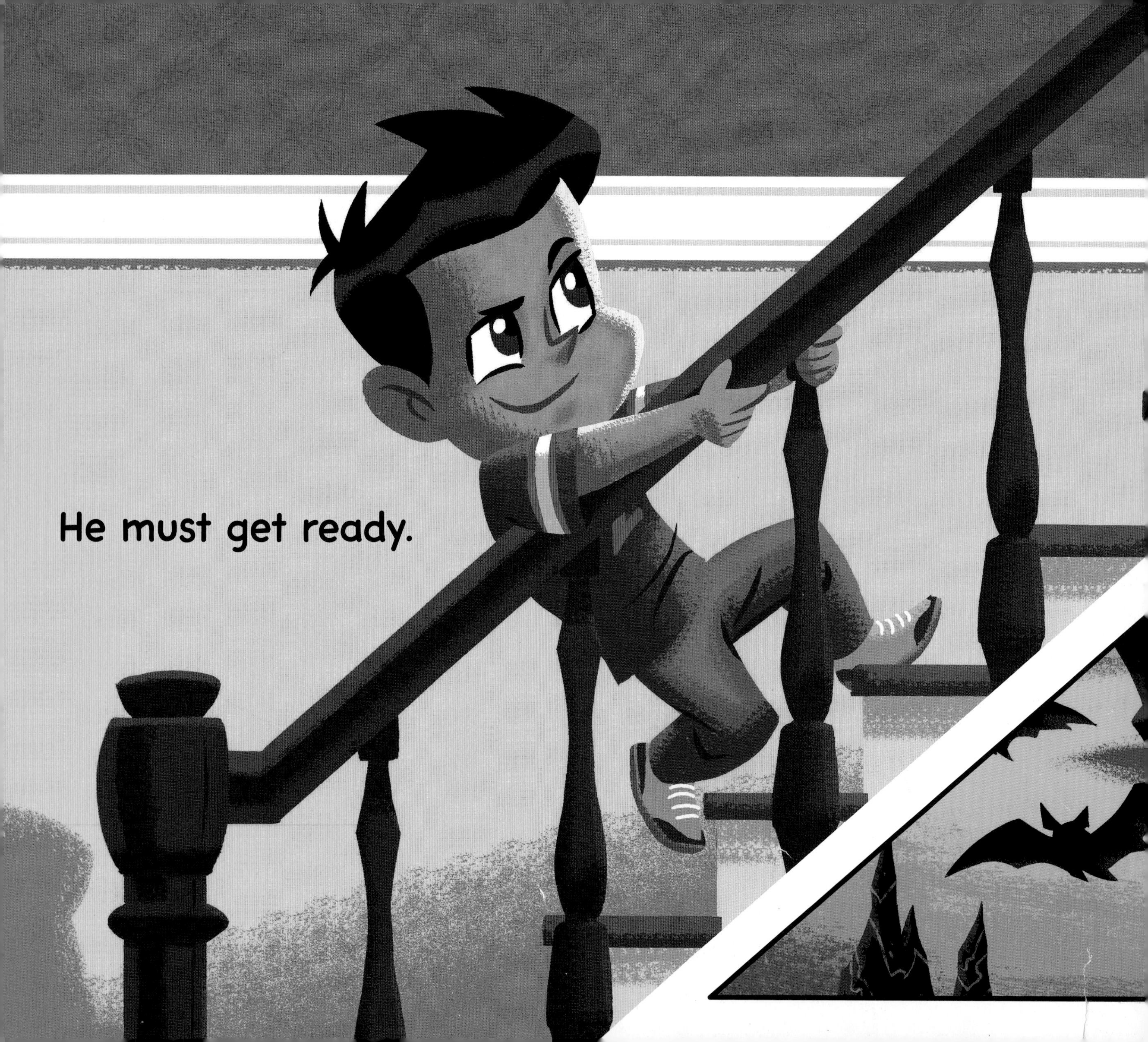

He must get ready.

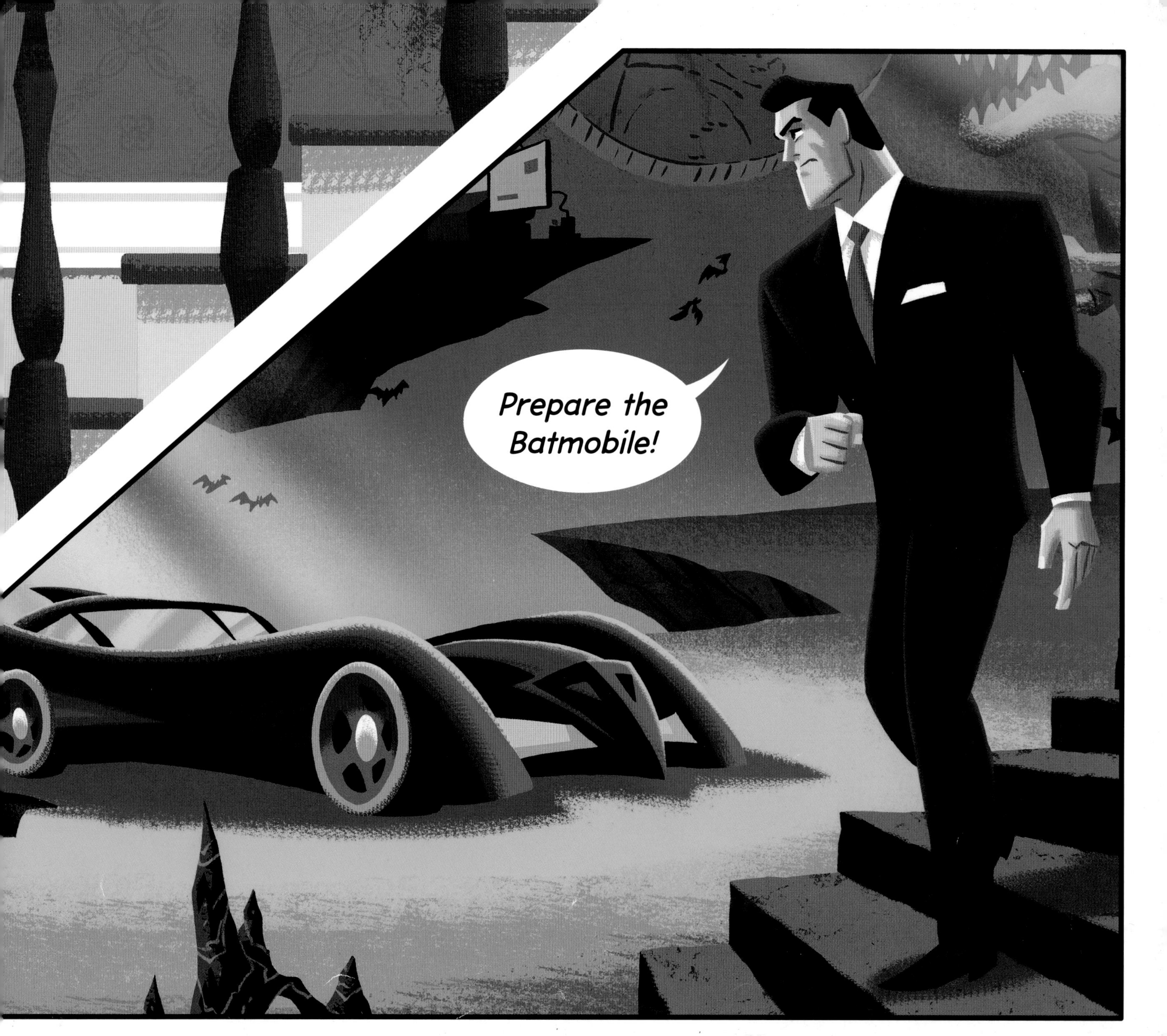
Prepare the Batmobile!

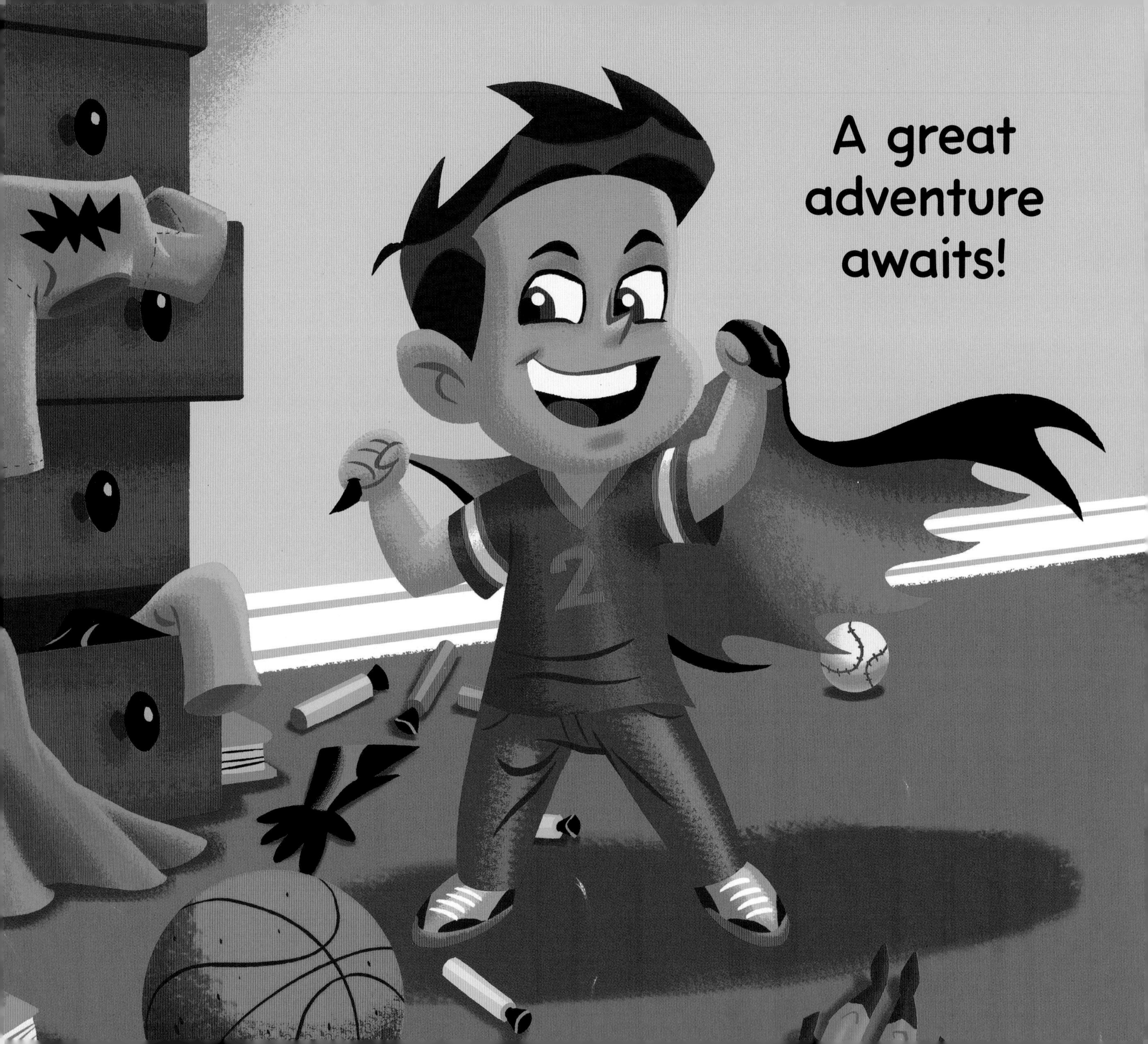

A great adventure awaits!

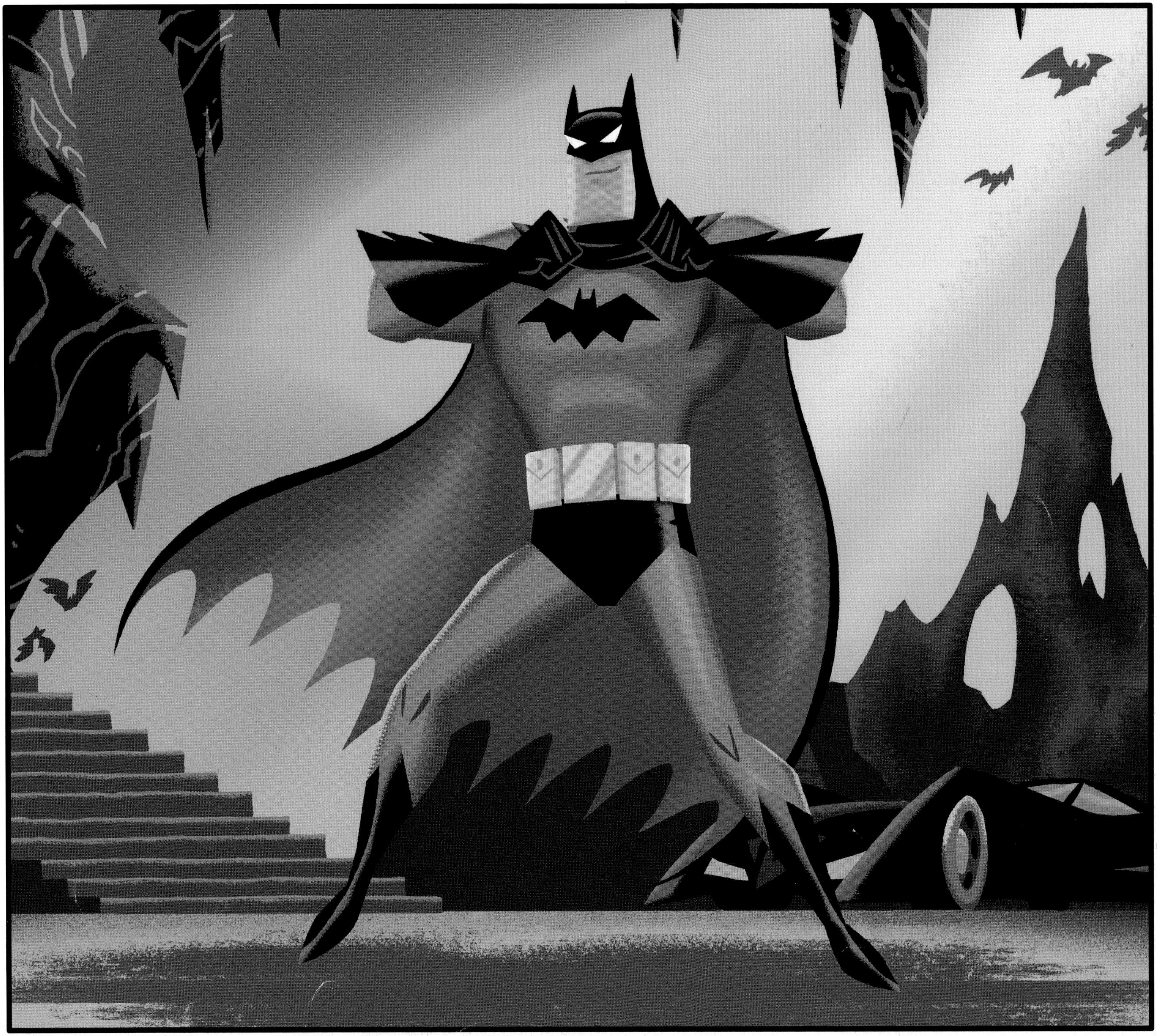

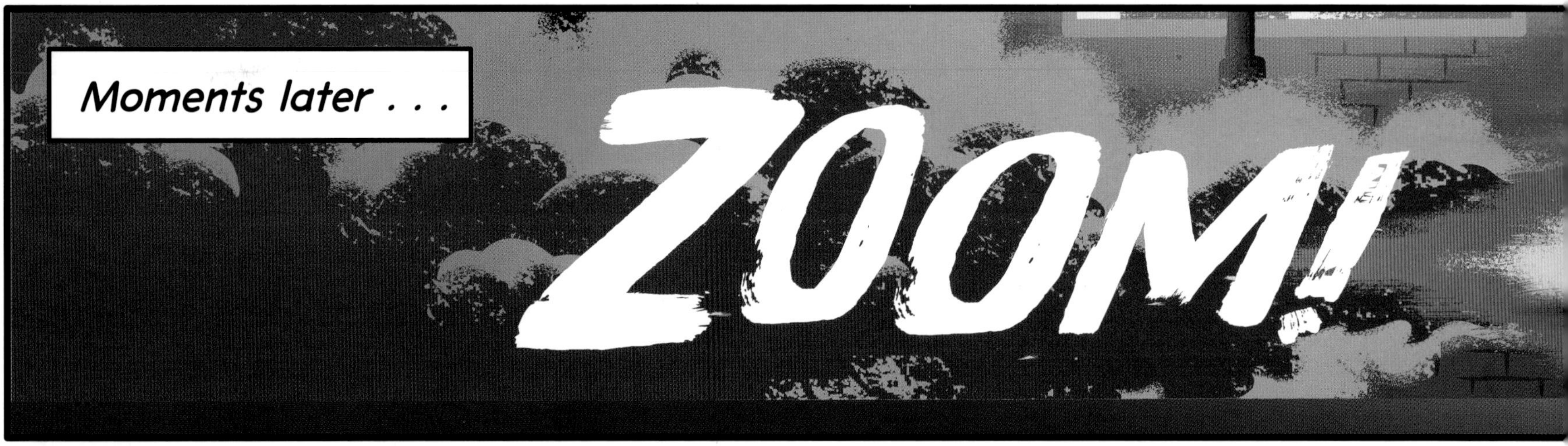
Moments later . . .
ZOOM!

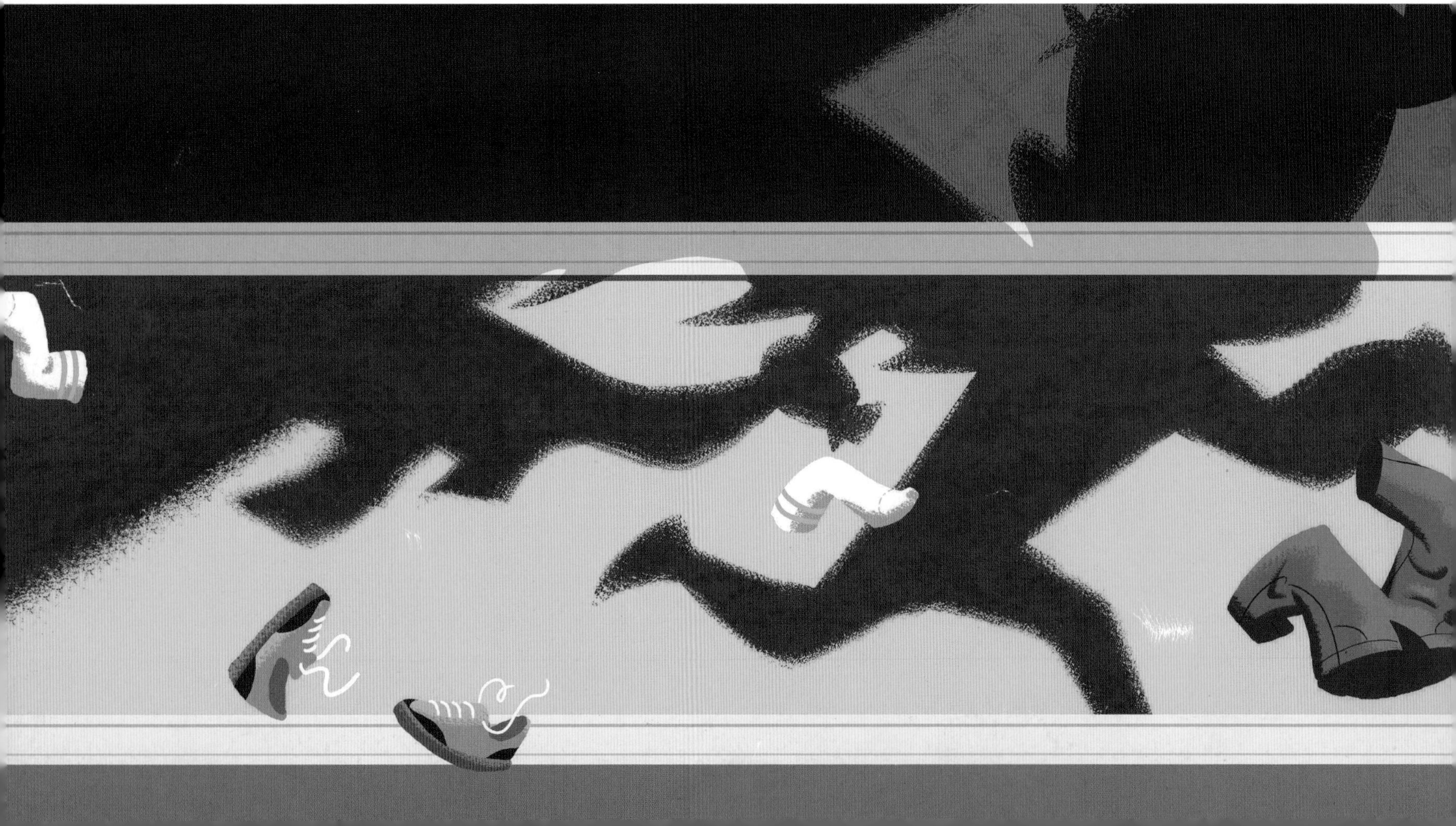

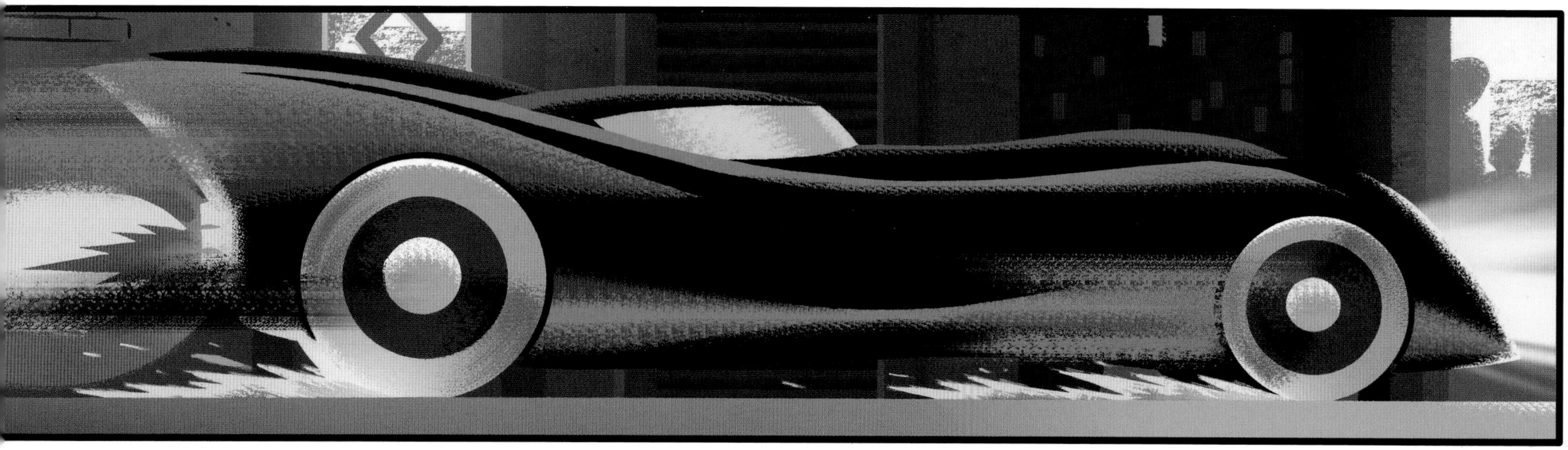

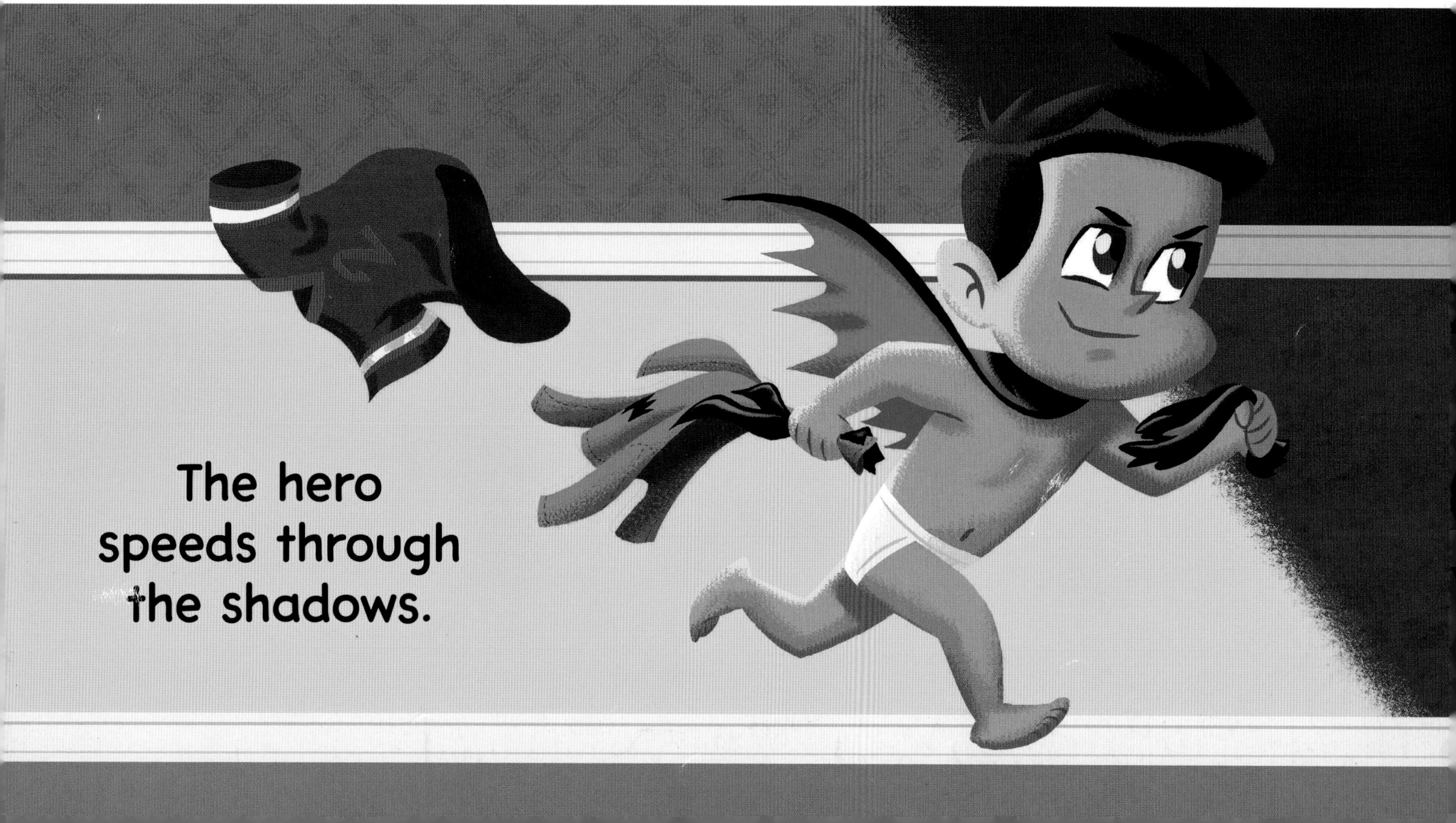

The hero
speeds through
the shadows.

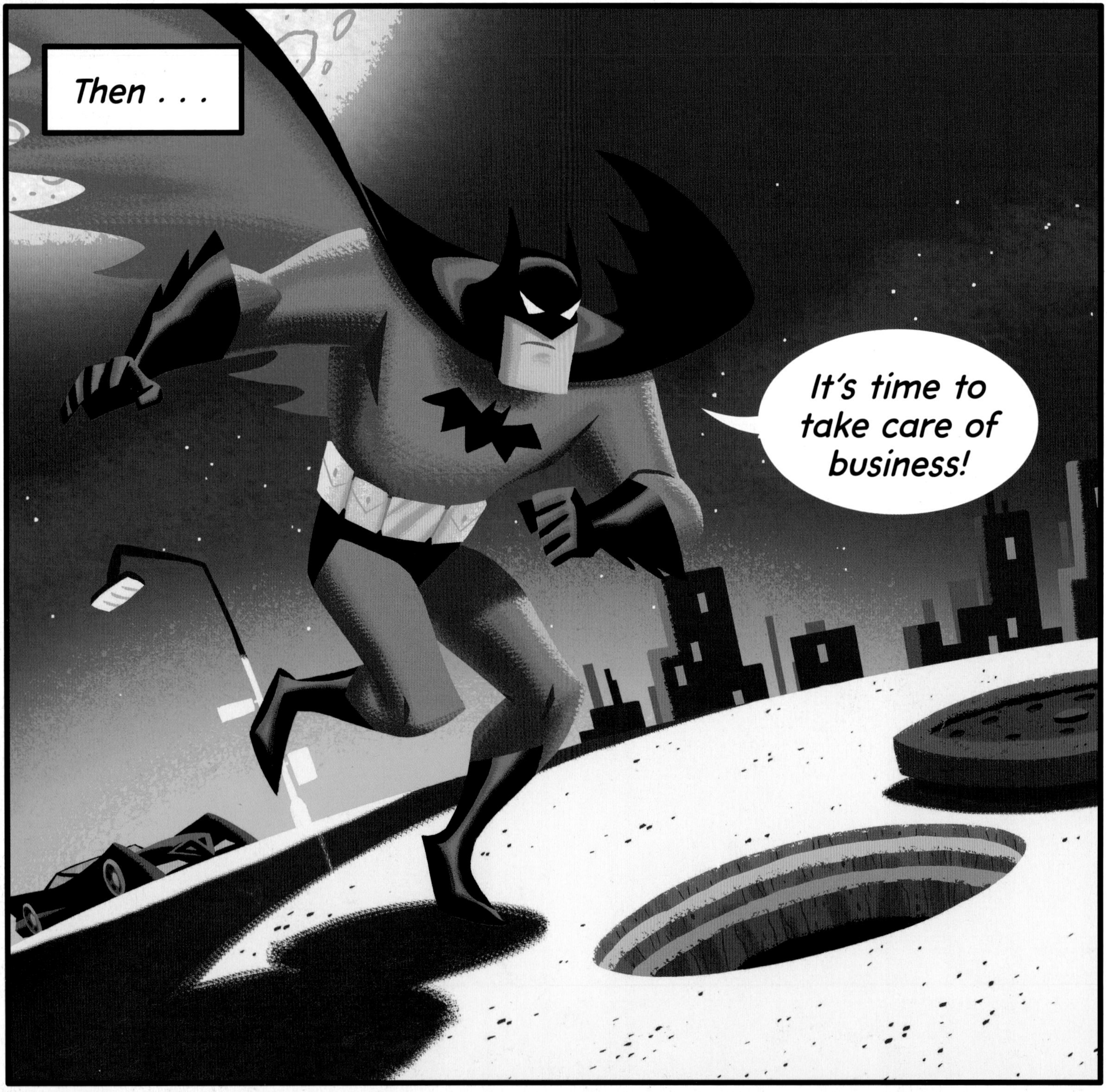
Then . . .
It's time to take care of business!

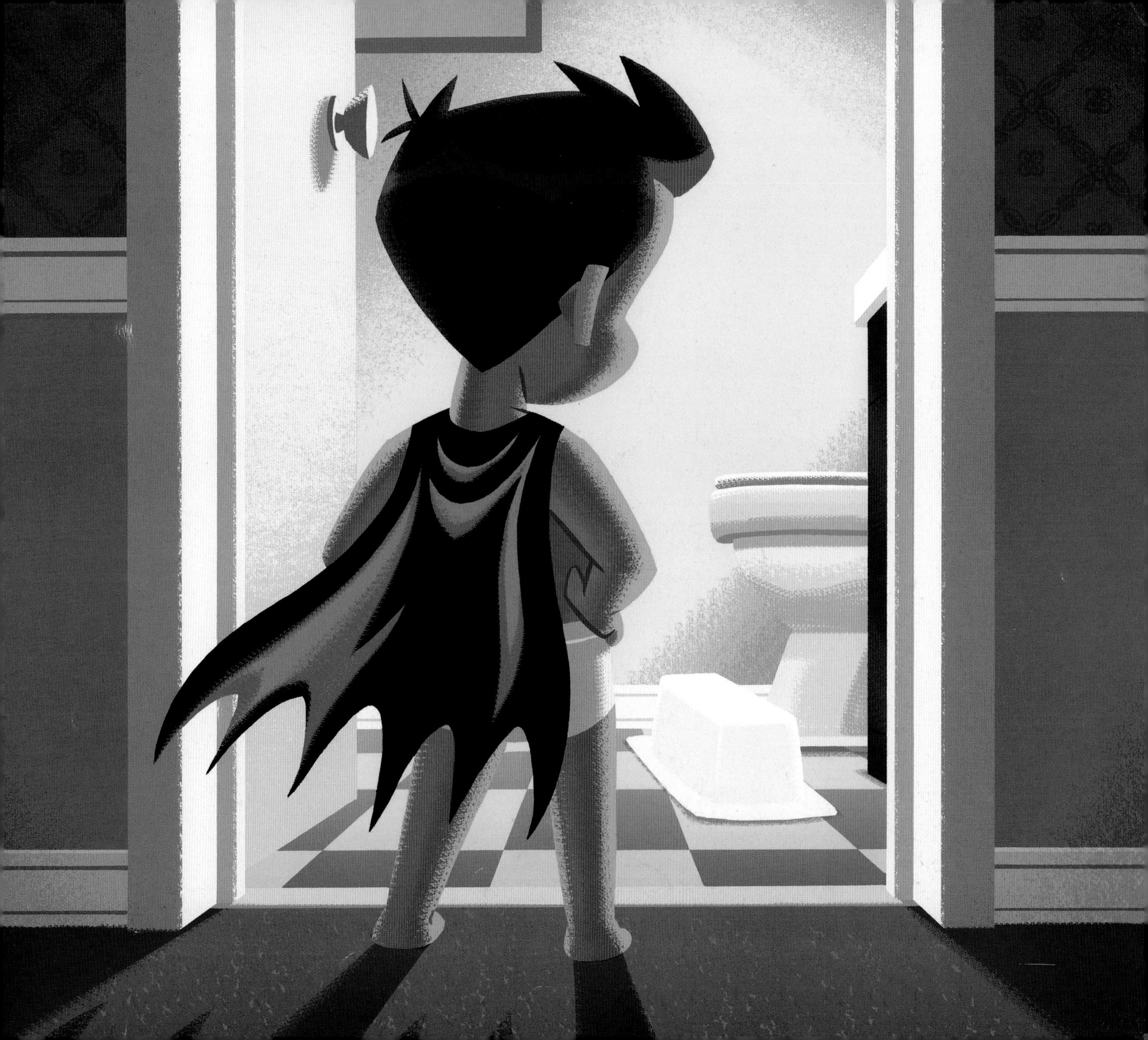

The hero cleans up the daily grime . . .

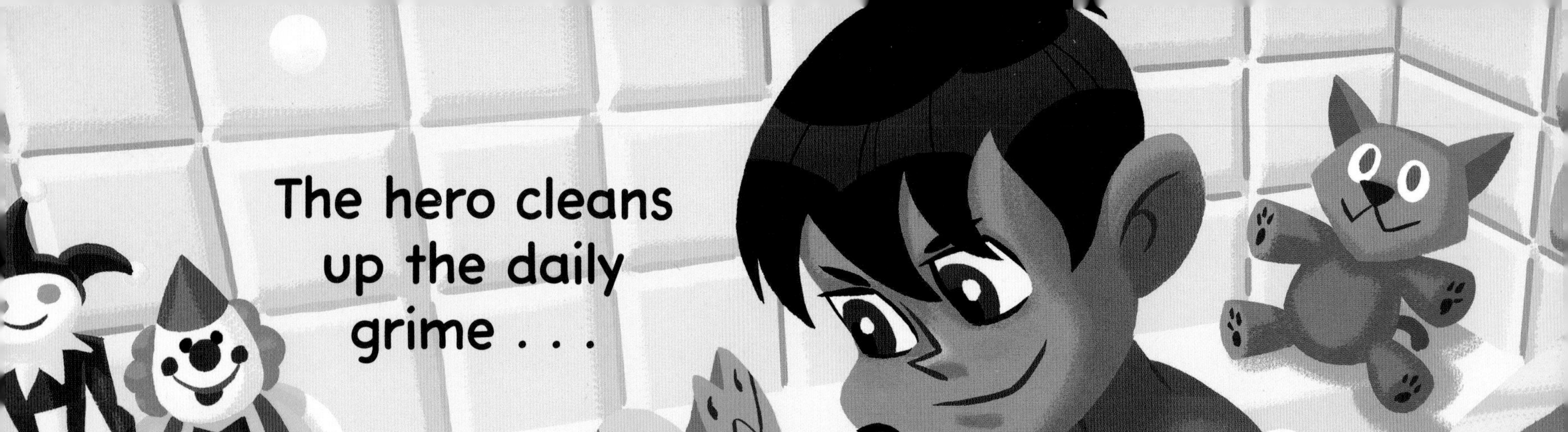

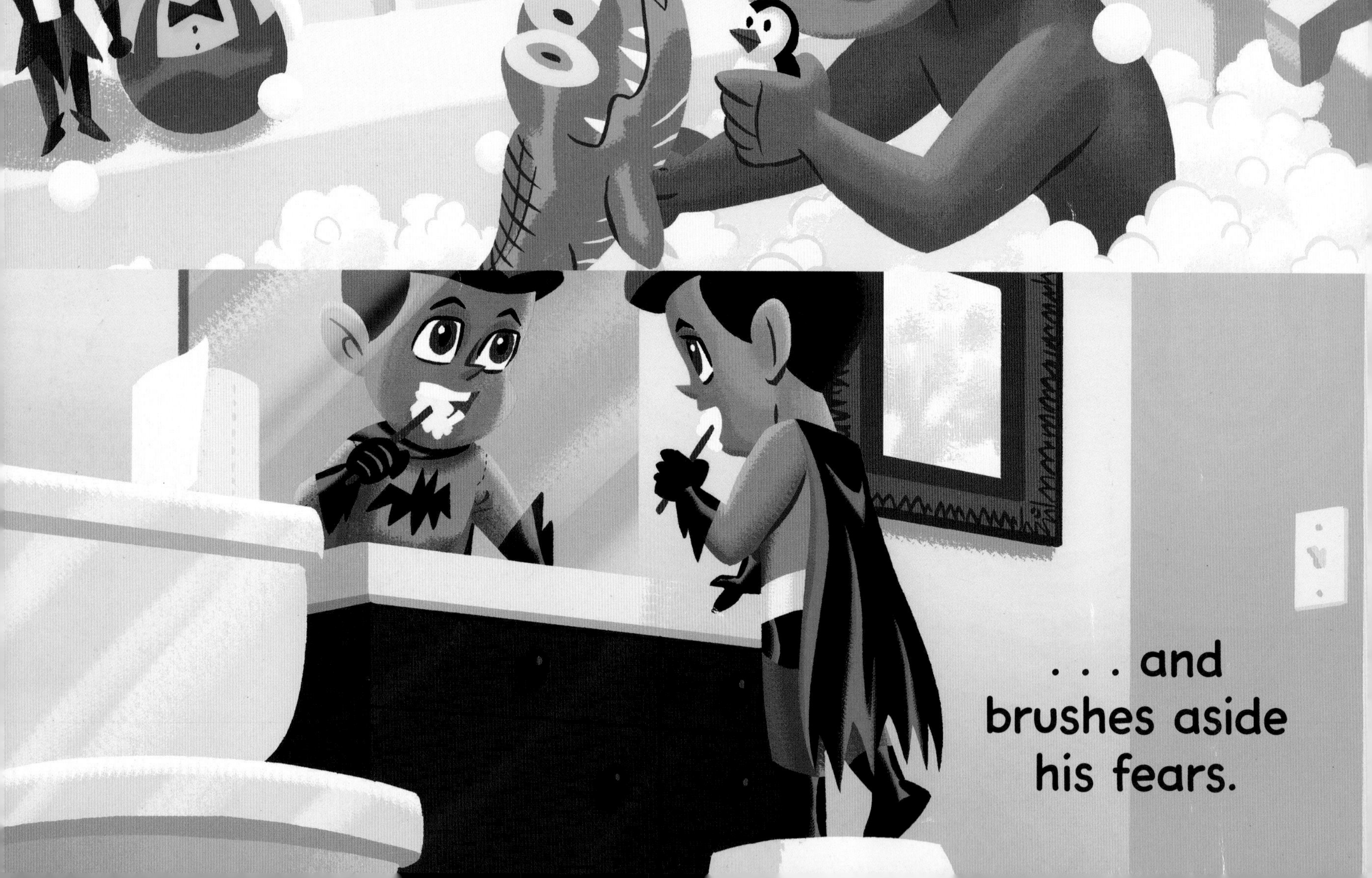

. . . and brushes aside his fears.

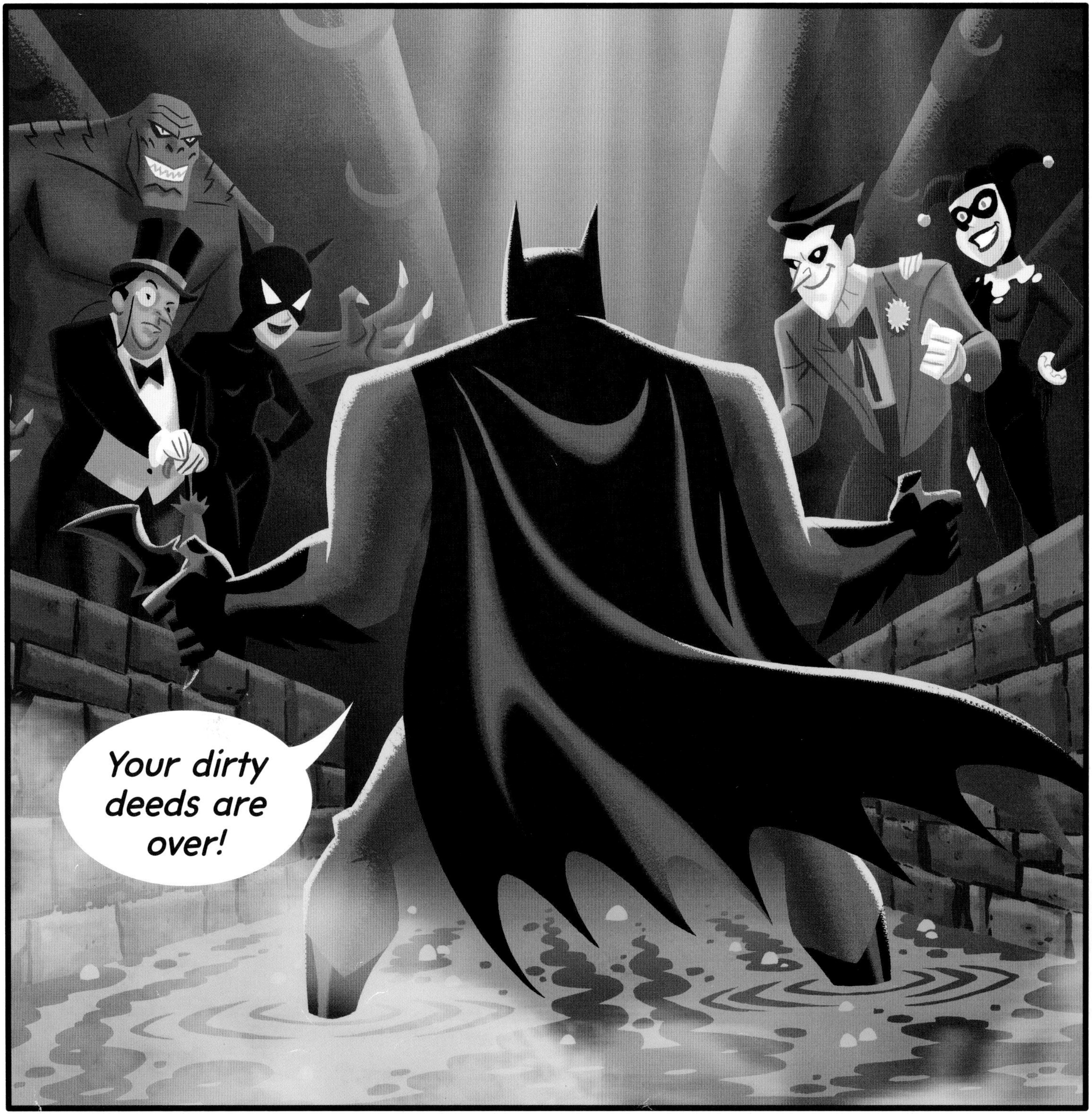
Your dirty deeds are over!

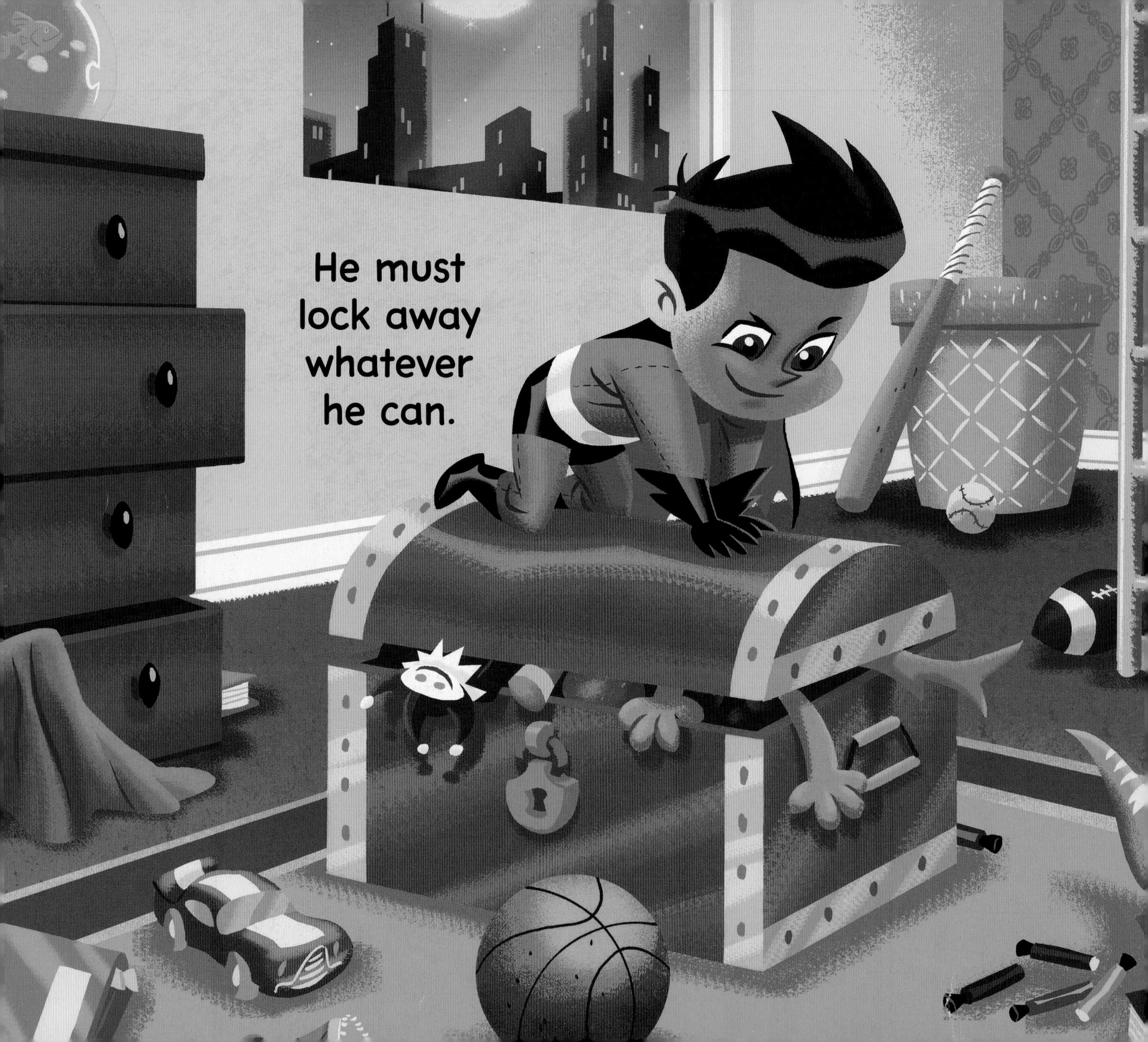

He must
lock away
whatever
he can.

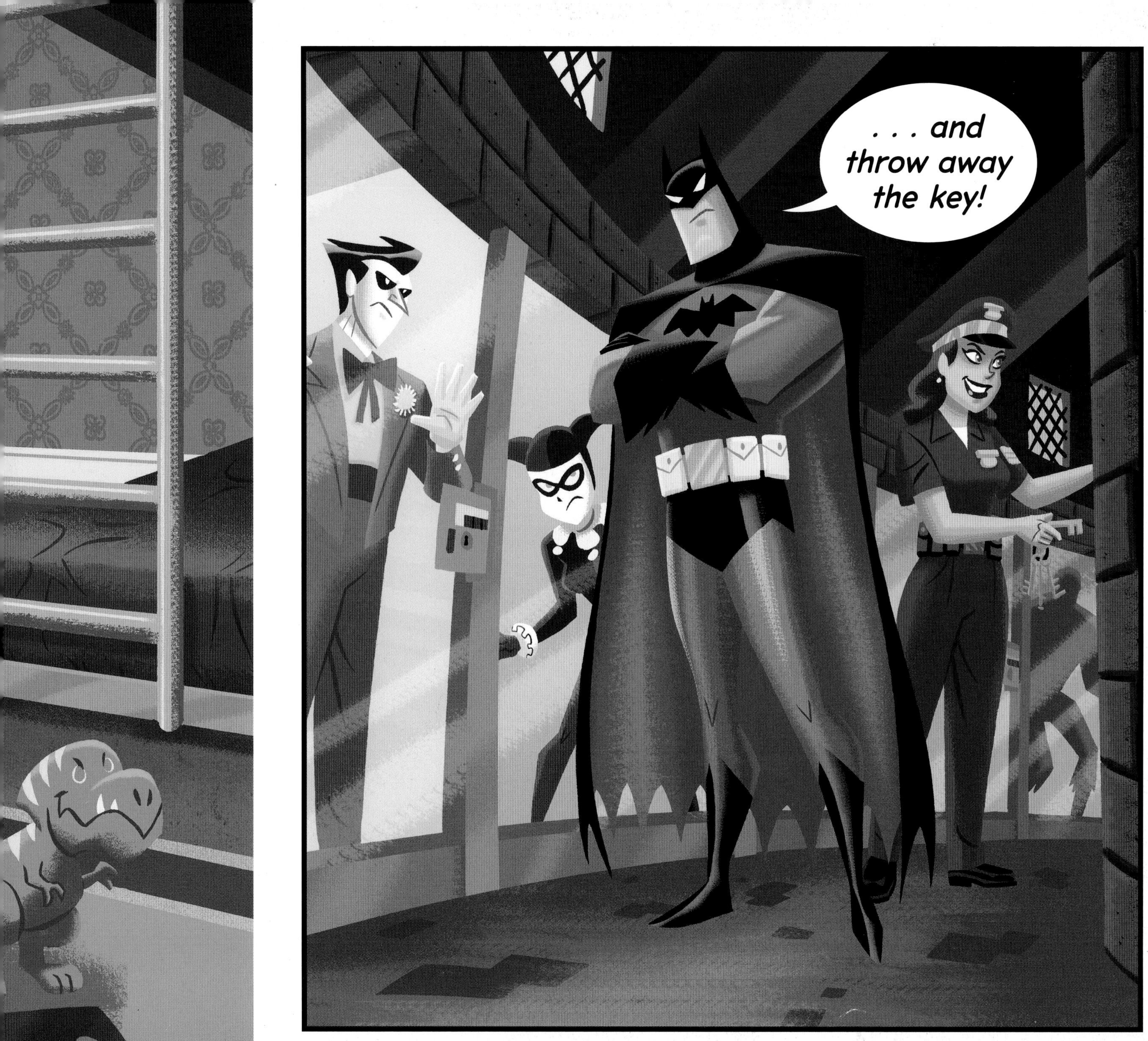
. . . and throw away the key!

For there are
those who depend
on him.

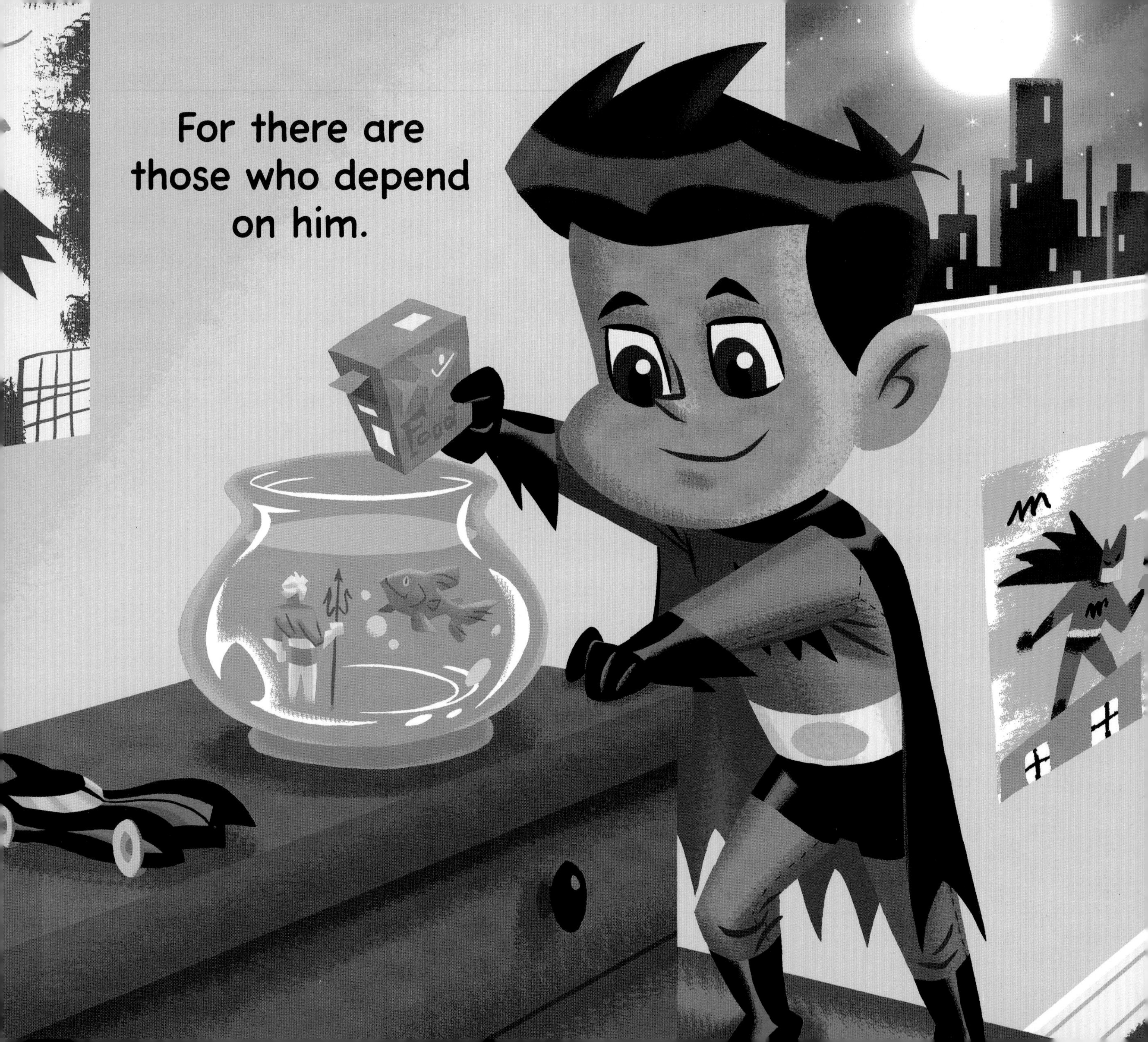
Food

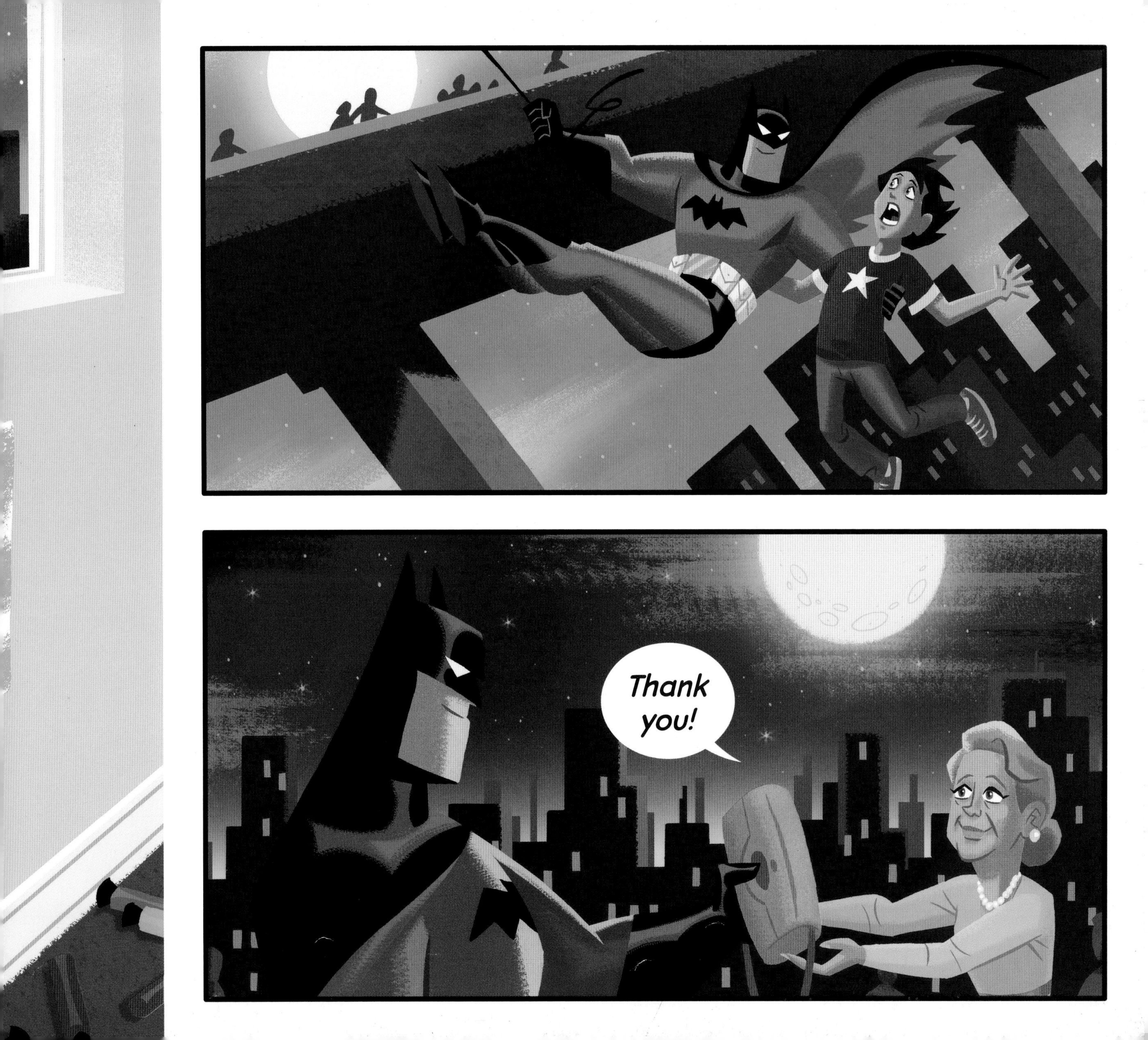
Thank you!

And those he
can count on.

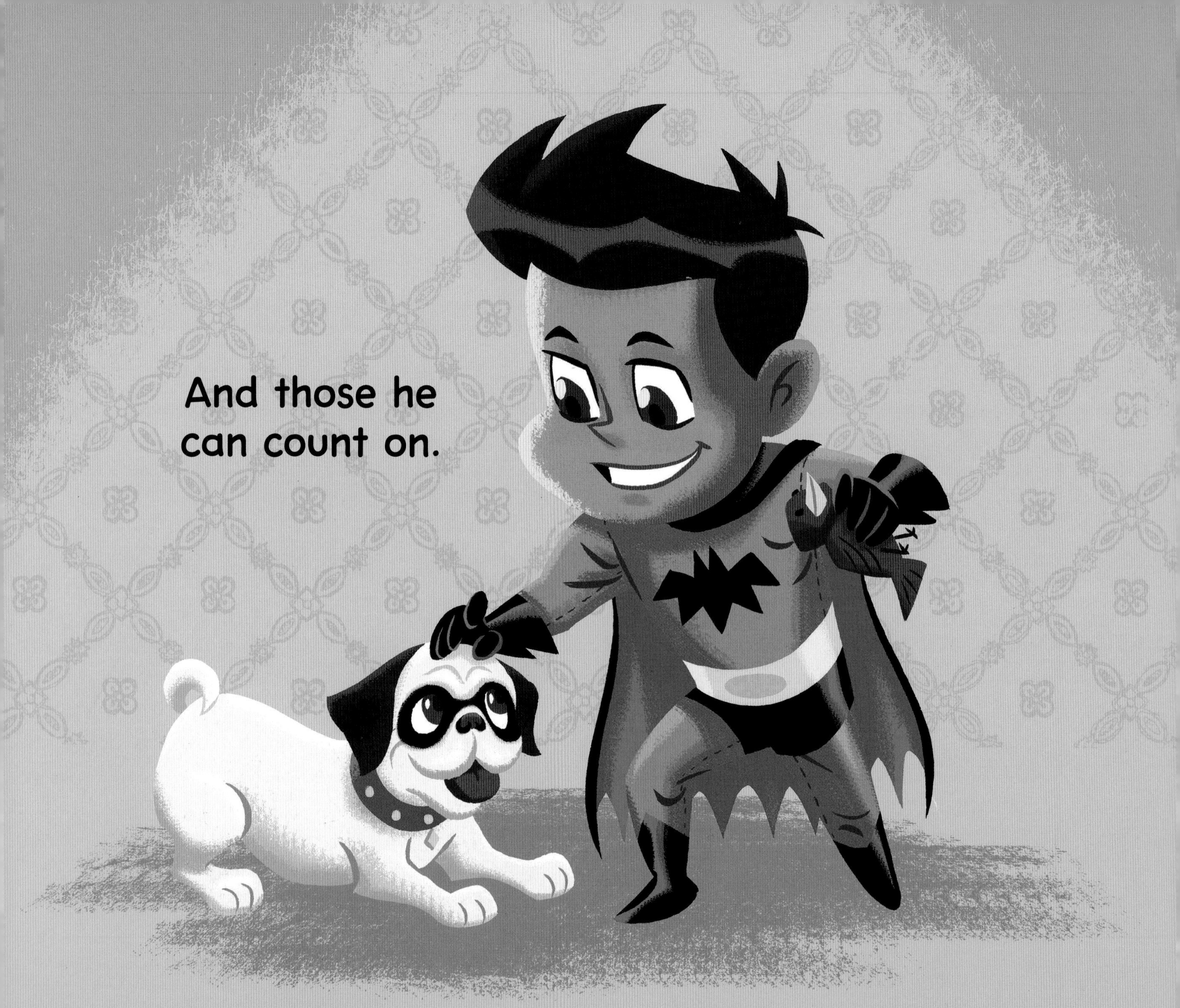

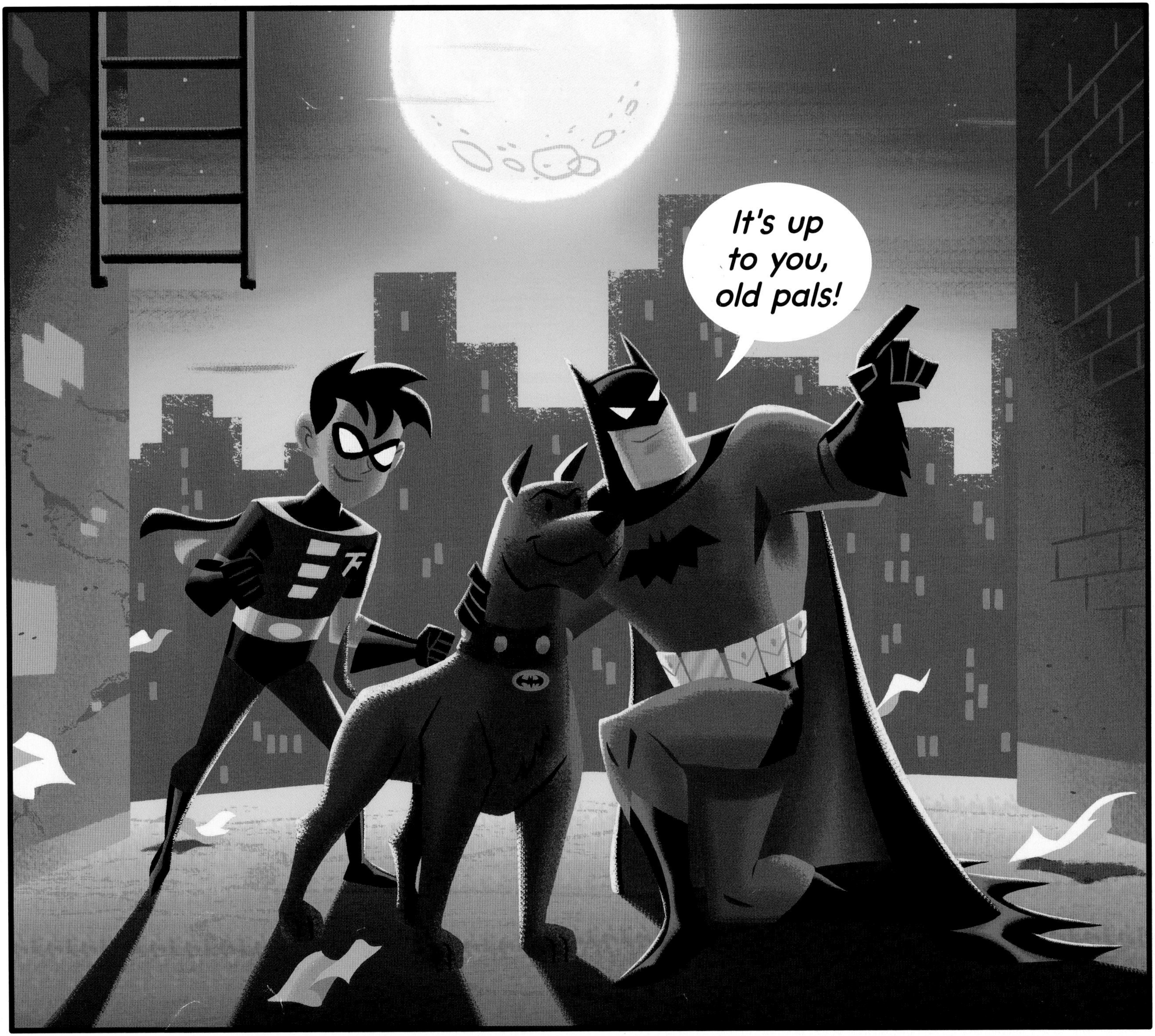
It's up to you, old pals!

The hero watches
over them all.

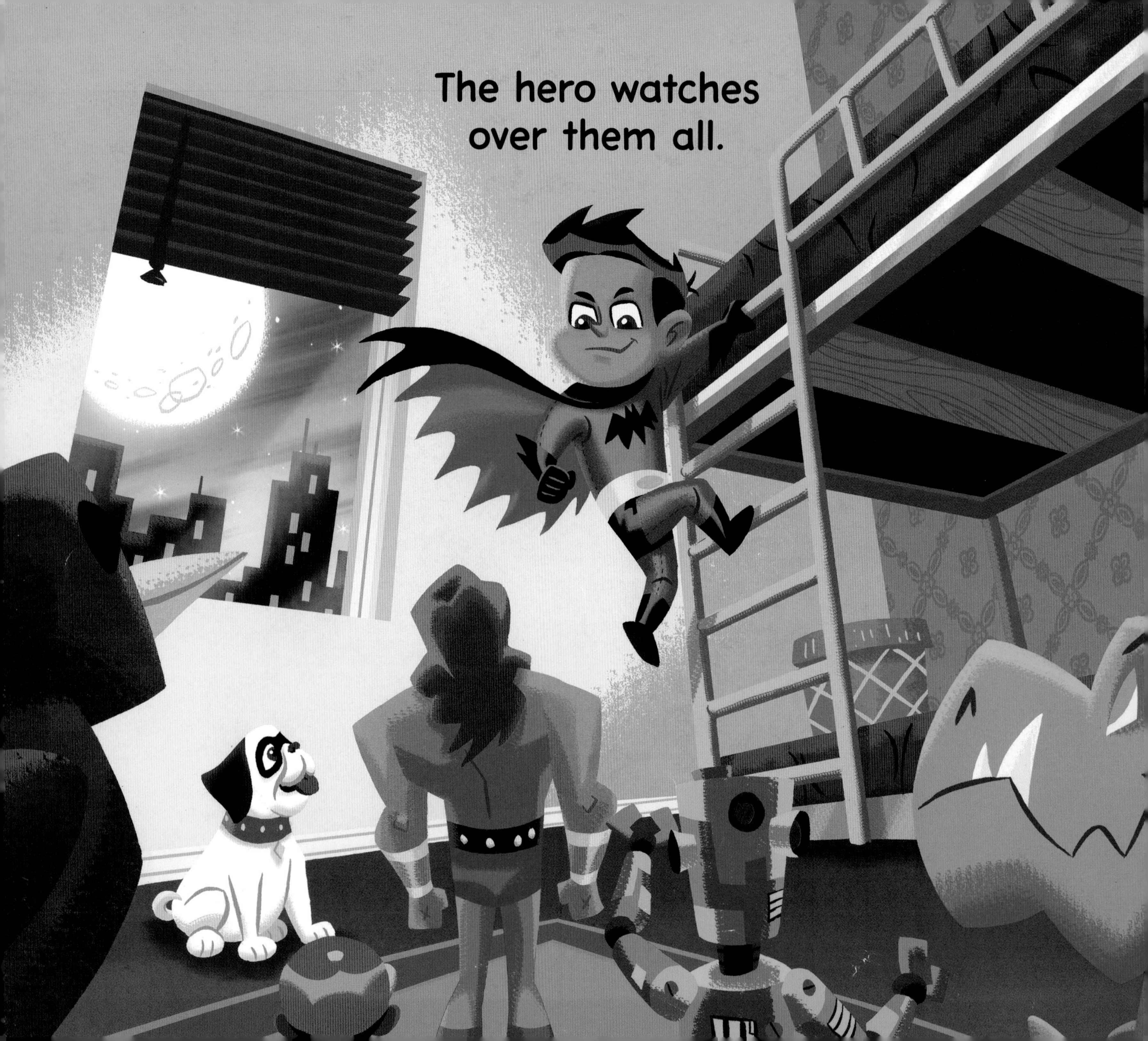

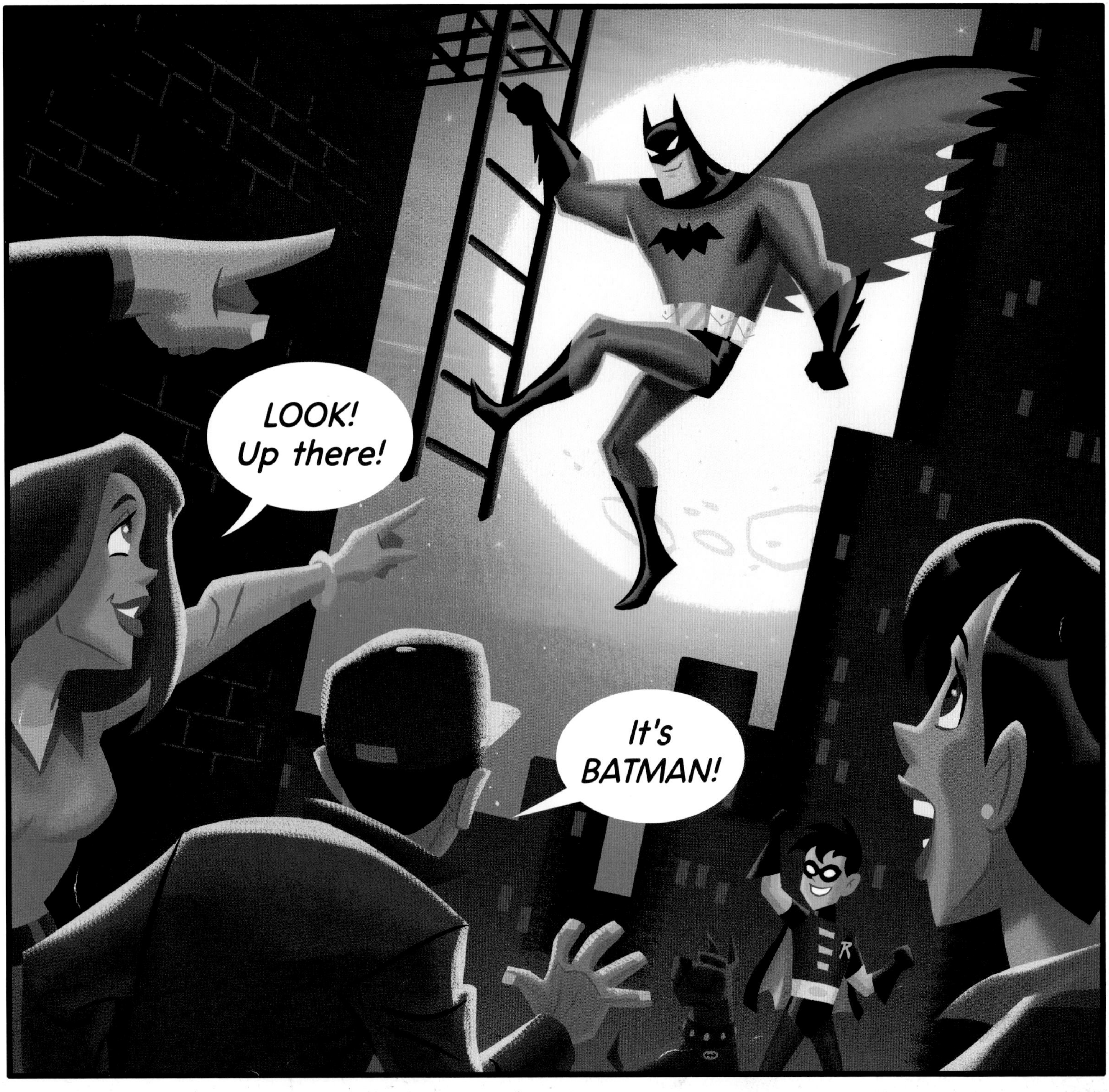
LOOK!
Up there!
It's
BATMAN!

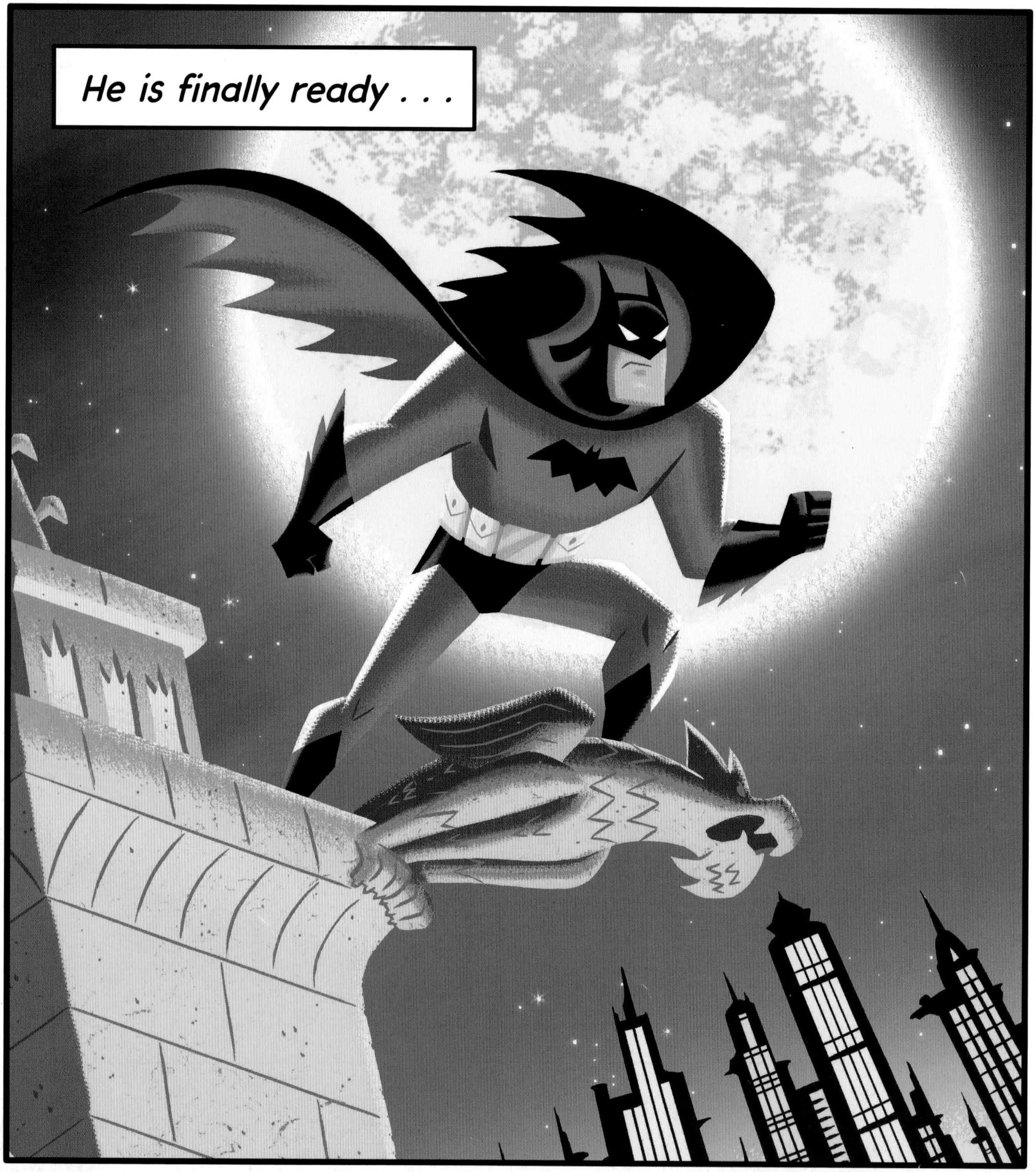
He is finally ready . . .

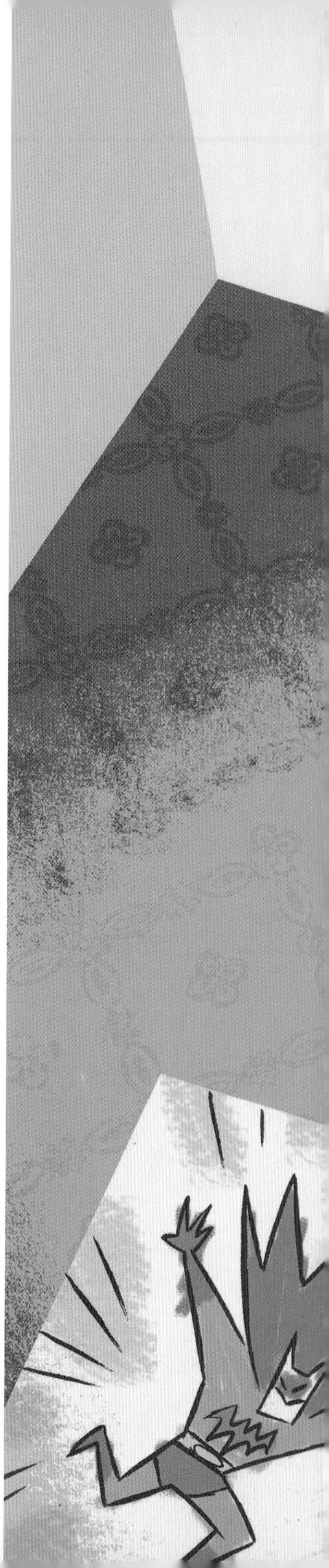

. . . for the
long night
ahead.

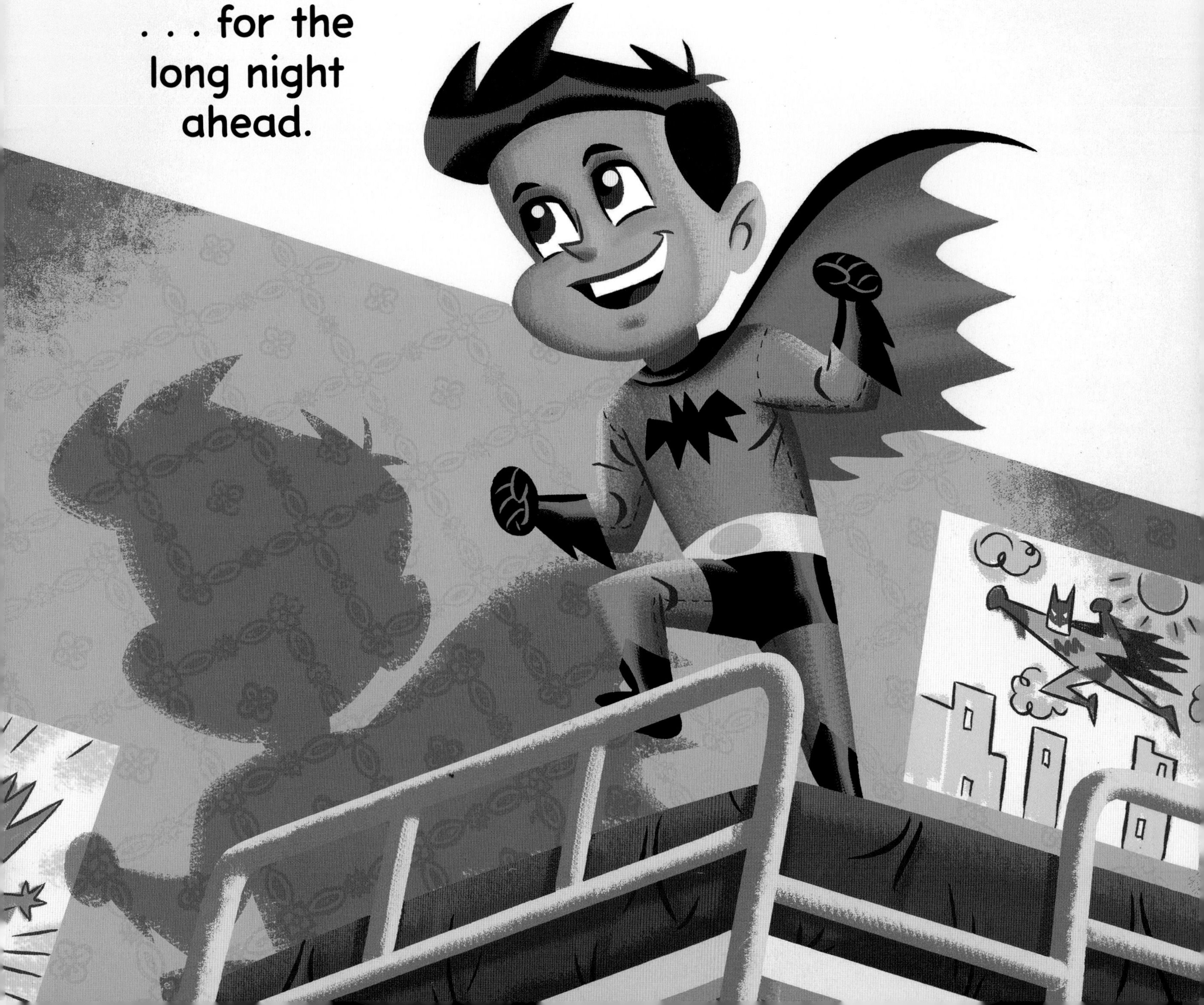

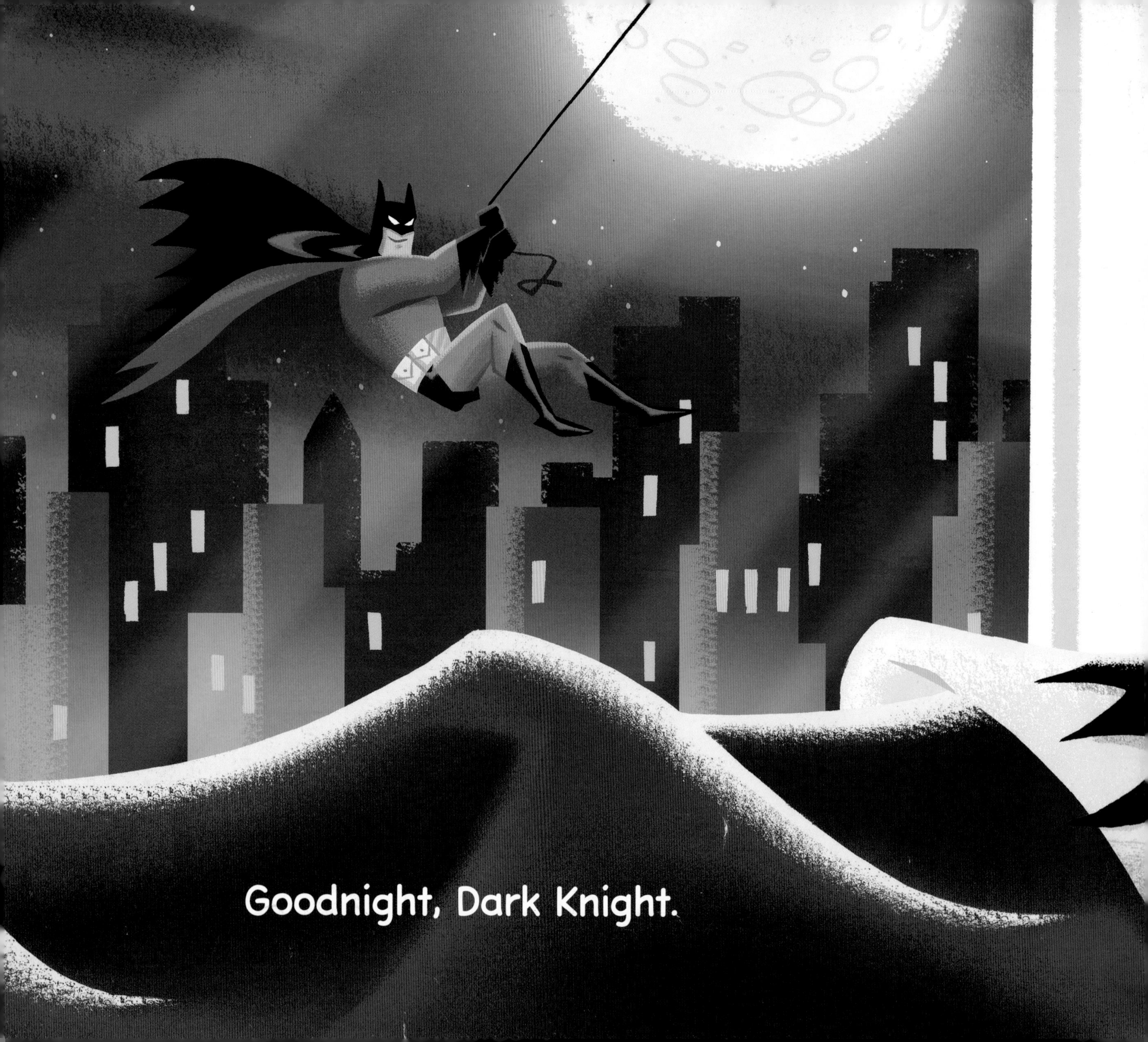

Goodnight, Dark Knight.

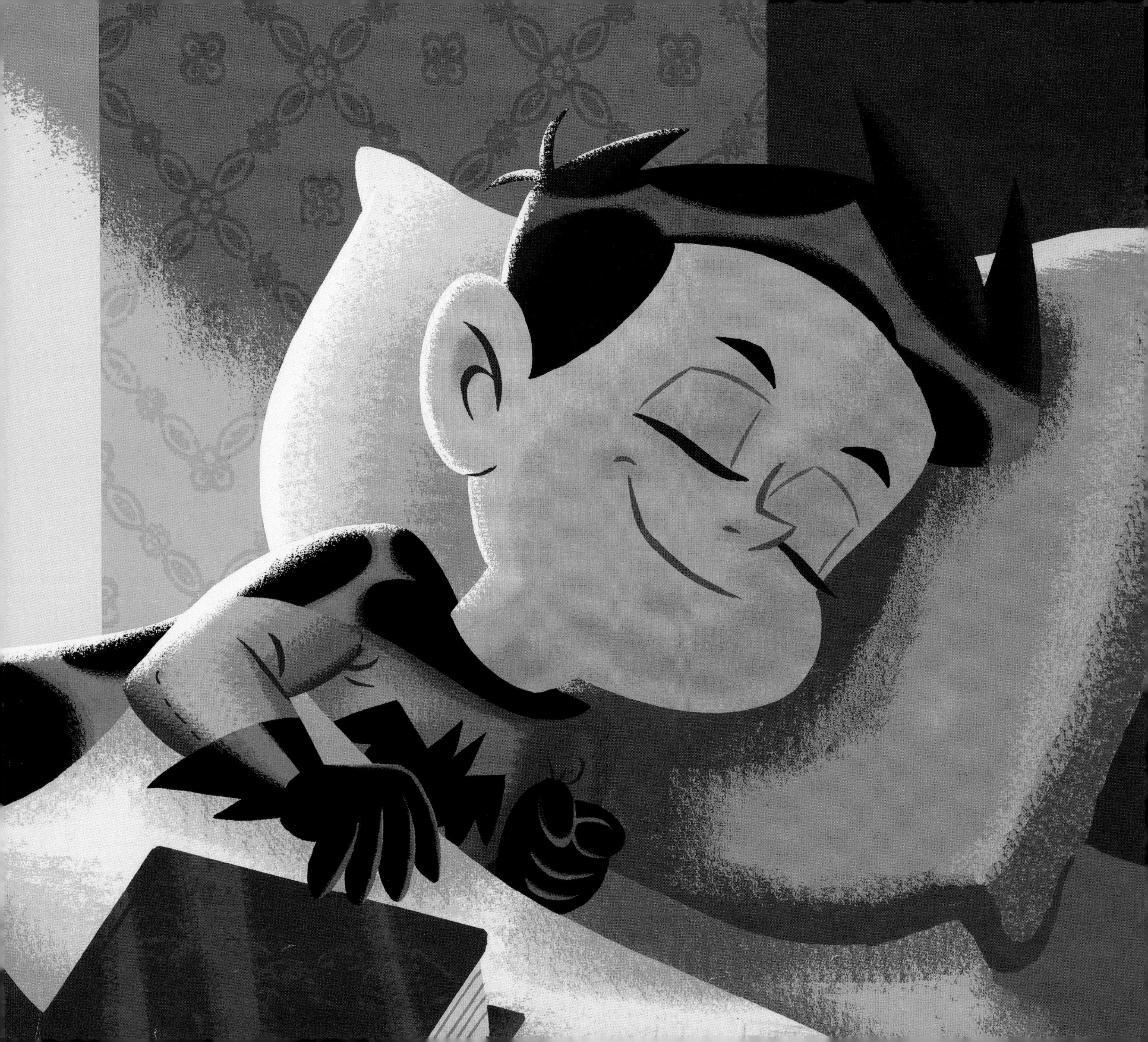

BEDTIME CHECKLIST!

Potty

Bath

Pajamas

Teeth

Pick up

Story time